THE WESTERN RAIDER:
GUN-CALL FOR THE LOST LEGION

GUN-CALL FOR
THE LOST LEGION

By Stone Cody

STEEGER BOOKS • 2020

CHAPTER 1
THE SIGN OF DISASTER

O N T H E edge of the town of Sangre de Cristo, a man in the ragged garb of a peon stood with his foot on a cask of wine, looking idly out toward the Sierras. All at once he caught his breath, stared.

His better-dressed companion turned on him crossly. "You look as though you had seen a ghost. What's the matter?"

The peon pointed silently.

"Well?" his companion insisted impatiently.

"The cloud... Do you not see?"

The sky was blue-hot and fleckless, and the cloud at which the peon had pointed was the only one visible. Dun colored, it looked at first glance like any other cloud might, sitting or rolling along one of the high, level, far-off ridges. But hardly a second glance was needed to see the remarkable resemblance it bore to something else. It had the perfectly formed shape of a cask of wine! But the eye caught something even more remarkable. The cloud was circled by darker bands—exactly like the hoops of a barrel... and at one end it was marked by a triangular patch of grayish white, as if this were the insignia of some wine grower painted on the barrel.

Mouth open in wonder, the second man looked down at the cask of wine from which the peon had now taken his foot. Then, quickly, he crossed himself. At one end of the barrel was

Silver's fist jabbed out as El Diablo arced his knife.

a triangular patch of white, dirtied to a dullish gray—matching with a preciseness that could not be overlooked, the gray triangle of the cloud!

The man swallowed hard, and looked back at the cloud. It was growing, had grown, even while he looked away from it. But as it grew it retained its shape. It remained a wine-cask, which now expanded darkly, ominously, against the flawless blue of the far sky.

The second man drew his breath deep and let it out in a long, tremulous sigh.

"It is a sign," he murmured, in awed superstition. "I wish I knew—" He broke off abruptly.

The cloud had begun to change its shape. The edges wavered, drew up. Fascinated, they watched, marking each slight change. Then the peon caught his breath sharply, and his brown face took on the color of a mildewed sheet.

"Madre de Dios!" he breathed.

Clearly it could be seen. The cloud had taken on the shape of a death's head! The gray which had marked the triangle had broken up to make pale hollow eyes and a grin of rooted teeth.

Then both the men were swallowing hard, and crossing themselves again.

Along the street, a party of countryfolk in holiday attire looked at them curiously.

"What ails you, *amigos?*" one of them called. "Has the good wine gone the wrong way down?"

A girl, pert on donkey back, added, "Let me make you some *enchilados* to clear your head. What will our Silver think if you show sick looks at his wedding?"

The second man's face darkened. He growled a sullen reply that changed the passer's-by holiday good-humor to scowls.

When they were gone, he turned on his still pale-faced companion with a ferocity born of deep unease.

"Idiot!" he snarled. "Have you no better business than to go sky gazing? You and your clouds! If I speak a word of this to—"

The ragged peon raised a finger to his lips in startled warning. *"Sh-h!"* he muttered. "Have we not bad luck enough without…."

"Bad luck?" The other glared at him. "How do you know it is

3

bad luck, *borrachon* without shame? How do you know it does not mean bad luck for this strutting fool who calls himself the Hawk and drips with holiness, though he is no more than an ordinary bandit like any other? It is his death—through this barrel—that your cloud predicts!"

Some of the color came back into the peon's face. He looked relieved.

"I had not thought of that," he murmured. Then his lips paled again. *"Dios!* But maybe it is our death, there in the sky—for who yet has clipped the wings of the Hawk?"

His companion's hand slid gently toward his knife. "Perhaps you are not of us," he murmured. "Can a servant of the Devil fear Hell?"

The peon's chest inflated suddenly with his sharp-drawn breath. But his hand also went toward his knife.

"Fool!" he said softly. "You are too stupid even to fear the good God. But not I! Draw your steel, species of fat dog! Or shall I cut your heart out, while you stand there like an overfed lizard?" **HIS HAND** flashed out, flicked forward. His companion's heavy eyes showed the desperation that moved his knife hand. But it was too late. The ragged peon's knife slid inward, between the ribs—a movement soft as the cutting of warm butter.

The man said "a-a-hh!" softly, and turned a long, hating look on the ragged peon. Then he slumped over the wine cask. Red cascaded from his heart, staining the gray-white triangle painted at the barrel's end.

Thus the cask of wine had its first baptism of blood.

The "peon" cast a sharp glance up and down the street. Nobody appeared to have noticed. A provident fate had arranged it so that none of the fiesta crowd was coming into town at that moment.

Swiftly, he seized the body of his companion and dragged him into the alleyway behind. Leaving him concealed by a pile of trash there, he returned to the wine-cask.

He had scarcely done so when a townsman appeared, pulling a two-wheeled cart, with himself between the shafts like a horse.

"What is sleep on a day like this?" the townsman asked in a low tone.

The peon who had killed drew a breath of relief. "Who sleeps is likely to meet death before he wakes," he replied.

The townsman nodded, throwing him a swift comprehending glance. Together, they lifted the cask of wine into the cart.

The townsman put himself between the shafts. "Begone, amigo," he whispered, "I would not care that any question you— if a certain thing should go wrong."

"He may be questioned," a grim voice said from the alley behind, "but I hardly think he will be in any condition to answer."

The peon stiffened. His breath became jagged. He turned his head slowly, and found himself looking into the heavy, jowled face of a man whose costume was that of a wine-grower, but whose sombrero jingled with conchas of a curious design, such as only one wine-grower in a thousand—and one with a very bold imagination—might have conceived.

"Back up, friend," the jowled man whispered. "Back up into the alley, without raising your hands, and don't make any noise."

The peon's Adam's apple worked hard, in a dry throat. There

was nothing for him to do but obey. He had seen the yawning black muzzle of the sixgun which now pointed exactly at the middle of his spine, and he had seen, too, the knife which glittered in the speaker's other hand.

He looked up the street, frantically, but there was no help there. Then he cast one yearning glance at the sky, and saw, far off, that the cloud he had seen was shapeless now, a mere funnel of black—a thunderhead—over the distant mountains.

He took another step backward, looked down and saw the body of his companion behind the trash. Complete understanding drove through him, and for one instant his whole being froze. He tensed, held motionless between his deadly need to cry some pleading word to the death behind him, and his knowledge that it would be useless—that he must risk everything on one lunging, hopeless flight.

Then the point of the knife slid between his ribs, and went inward with so little feeling that he could barely believe his own keyed senses until the hilt of it stumped against his back. Silently, almost, he slumped onto the refuse pile beside the body of his companion.

THE JOWLED man laughed a little, a note of satisfaction in his tone, on seeing that the peon's body had fallen almost exactly on his dead companion—which was exactly as he had planned. Then he snapped to the staring-eyed townsman, "Go on. And see that there is no more bungling today!"

The wine-drawer moved swiftly, dragging the cart behind him. He went down the street, never unconscious of the jowled, paunchy figure that followed him, an unvarying twenty paces behind.

After a little, he came into populous streets. A motley and hilarious crowd of celebrants swarmed in and out of the cantinas and upon the walks. Color and gaiety swirled and eddied about him everywhere.

This was a day of fiesta such as Sangre de Cristo had not known before. This was Silver Trent's wedding day, and a whole countryside had gathered to do honor to him and his bride. Peons and their wives from the *campagna, vaqueros* and their chosen girl friends, small farmers, villagers, goat herders from lonely spots in the hills, prospectors, hunters, trappers—all had converged on Sangre for this day.

It was a queer and ironic situation—this celebration of an outlaw's wedding. Silver Trent had incurred the hatred of the rich, and there was a price on his head on both sides of the Border. Yet though there were federal troops and a "loyal" government in this town of Sangre, Trent and his Hawks walked free. Even the *Rurales*, ordinarily tough and fearless men, would not dare try to arrest him. For this was a celebration of the poor and underprivileged, and to them the outlaw was very nearly a God. A good proportion of them had fought under his command on that great day when he had broken the power of Esteban Varro and saved the countryside from a hell's reign of injustice and oppression. Now it would require an army to arrest Silver Trent here—or to arrest the least of his men!

No known enemy of Silver Trent's could live long among that loyal and worshiping throng, but a cask of wine could go through without a challenge. More! It could meet cheers and joyous shouts along the way.

"*Hola!* A cask of the great wine of Cerridos!" someone called. "Have you brought it for me and my *señorita, hombre?*"

"And is this your wedding, *amigo?* If the saints wish it, you shall have such wine for the birth of your seventh son!"

The wine-drawer answered so with forced geniality, hoping, with a certain cold spot in the small of his back, that the ears of his jowled escort approved.

Then, suddenly, a grinning giant, flanked by carnival celebrants on either side, blocked the carter's way. "*Bueno, hombre! Basta!* You have gone far enough. Unload the cask."

The wine-carter stopped short. His lips parted in an uneasy and obsequious smile, while the hairs along the back of his neck lifted. These were men of the Hawk. He knew them. Ricardo of the swagger and the lean, sunlit face—which reminded one of a smiling, good-humored wolf. The *medico-americano*, Doc Brimstone, with his hearty belly and his great, empurpled beak of a nose. And a man with a wooden leg, who had a circumference and a proboscis to outrival the doctor—Big Nose Beaujolais. This one had lost his leg in Silver's service, but on his oaken peg, he was still a match for half a dozen ordinary fighters.

"*Señores,*" the carter said, dry-throated, "this wine is for the great *Halcon* himself—a wedding present from the wine-makers of Cerridos. It is of the oldest and best."

"*Hola!*" cried Doc Brimstone, smacking his lips. "Then it is for us, also. Come along, *compadre*. You shall have a guard of honor." LAUGHING, THE three fell in beside the carter, helping

Silver Trent

him through the crowd. The wine-drawer put his head down and pulled, keeping a steady pace, thanking whatever saints he had that these three were too lordly drunken to observe the pallor of his face and the fear which flecked his eyes.

What was happening was great good luck for those who had sent the wine, but it was not such good luck for him. No one would ask questions now. There could be no possible suspicion of this cask, since it came under this escort. But also, the carter knew, there was no longer any chance for him to slide away unrecognized and soon forgotten.

No matter what happened now, he would be a marked man, to be run down and to be flayed alive when caught. Sheer, screaming panic crawled within him. For a cent, for a whisper, for a sharp word in his ear, he would have dropped the cart-handles

9

and run for his life. Only, there was a certain jowled man behind him, whose work with a knife he had already seen.

The carter plodded on silently, cold rivers of sweat running down his body under his clothes.

Blood, he knew, would soon flow free. Much blood....

CHAPTER 2
FIESTA OF DEATH

THE COLOR and gaiety of the fiesta took on a night-mare quality for the carter. Everything blurred before his eyes—the great barbecue pits, where whole steers and sheep and goats and pigs roasted and beer and wine kegs flowed in a continuous stream; the roistering geniality of the cantinas and restaurants, where everyone was invited to eat and drink his fill at El Halcon's expense; the swirling, interweaving, laughing crowds. All this seemed, suddenly, to him, a *danse macabre* for the imminent funeral of one poor wine carter.

Then they were there, at the great hall next door to the church, where Silver's men were gathering for their leader's wedding breakfast.

Shaking, the drawer got the barrel down from the cart and rolled it into the great room.

"Old wine of Cerridos, *compadres!*" Doc Brimstone boomed from the doorway. "The best in the land."

A shout of raillery and acclaim greeted him from the men who lounged about the great table spread for the wedding break-fast. They made a sight there, these men of the Hawk. Lean-limbed or heavy, sprawling, gesticulating, relaxed, they bore a queer, intangible mark in common—not so much the brand of the wolf, as a certain fierce yet genial ease which was native to the sort Silver Trent picked to ride with him. Men to whom fear was a stranger. Whose laughter rang free of all anxiety. Who bent their backs to no one and thumbed their noses where they willed. Fighting men. Who could be implacable foes, but who were not afraid to be friends, with all the obligations true friendship might imply.

The single, curious, hard-bitten character of them was written in the easy freedom of their gestures, the frank, untroubled glances of their eyes, the spontaneous merriment that ran along their mingled voices. And there was something else, too that marked them—a strange, underlying deadliness, a danger, such as one might feel in a lazing pack of wolves or a playful group of mountain cats.

These were the men of the Hawk….

Among them, only one stood out as a seeming alien—Pablo the Pious, whose only drunkenness was war. Liquor seemed not to affect him, other than to increase the fanatical melancholy of his worship of the saints, and augment the piety which blazed along the lines of a face which had the emaciated, upward-burning features which El Greco loved so to paint. There was little difference between him drunk and sober, except that, drunken, he might resent a sacrilege more violently. Yet in battle, he turned into a cursing madman whose inspired and gargantuan blasphemies had become a legend in the land.

He alone sat melancholy and brooding, as if some vague hint of trouble disturbed him.

"More wine and less sense!" he muttered. "If you were not so drowned in liquor, you might have seen the face that I have seen this day in Sangre."

Beside him, a huge, blond man with shoulders like the Bull of Bashan turned a pair of tawny, leonine eyes upon him. "What's that, old friend?" he grinned. "More grumbling?"

This was Lars Johanssen, bigger than Silver himself, though his great muscles lacked a shade of the flickering dynamite which lived in his leader.

"Too much for your fuzzy head," Pablo told him acidly. "Like the others, you can see nothing beyond your nose. Because we are in a town where nine men out of ten would give their lives for Silver, you think there is no danger. El Diablo, I tell you, still lives, and while he lives...."

"You are right!" Lars bellowed, his eyes glinting humor. "You mus' make a speech about it, Old Wolf. Ve haf not had a speech since t'ree minutes!"

In a movement surprisingly graceful in so big a man, he slid out of his chair. He placed his hands under Pablo's armpits and lifted him onto the table as easily as though he had been a child. **IT WAS** a movement unbelievably swift and unexpected. Yet when Pablo landed, cat-footed and twisting on the laden board, the naked blade of his knife was at Lars' great throat, the point of it tickling the skin.

"And now, *amigo,* will you move some more?" the Mexican grinned.

12

The huge Swede grinned back at him, holding carefully motionless. "Hell!" he said, "I ban scairt to breathe. Go make your speech, an' tak' your sticker away from my Adam's apple."

Pablo took the knife away and turned to the crowd that was lounging at the table and tossing jokes and laughter at him.

"Laugh!" he said scornfully. "Laugh and get yourselves drunker. You think you are safe, don't you? Go ahead and get yourselves helpless with wine. Maybe you will wake up with a head, and maybe—you will not wake up at all!"

"Listen to him!" Magpie Myers yelled, his eyes twinkling in his ageless, wrinkled-heather face. "You'd think he never took a drink."

"I can carry my liquor," Pablo retorted. "I don't see any signs that you can do the same."

A blocky, green-eyed youngster with reddish hair sat up in pretended indignation. He slapped his glass of *tequila* down on the table in front of him.

"You think I'm too drunk to take care of myself?" he challenged. "Then keep your eye on your hat, my old praying compadre!"

His right hand blurred to his thigh, whipped up, iron-freighted. The movement was so fast that the eye could not follow it—until the eared-back hammer of the sixgun slapped downward and the gun spat flame, roaring.

Pablo had hung his hat by its chin-strap on a peg on the wall behind him. As the shot rang out, the chin-strap was severed half an inch from the peg.

It was gunplay so blindingly fast and accurate that only Jim

Clane, or possibly Beau Buchanan, of all that crowd, would be capable of it. Though Silver himself, it was known, could shade even Jim and Beau, in the speed of his draw, and could still give them odds in marksmanship. But this gunplay was fast and sweet enough to draw yells of admiration even from the master gunmen in that crowd.

The yells burst out, stopped dead short, and then began again, mingled with appreciative laughter. For another man at that table had moved—Ricardo, who had helped bring in the wine.

Ricardo's hand had moved with a speed equal to Jim's, but toward a knife instead of a gun. The blade of it gleamed an instant in the air and then clunked into the wall, quivering, and the hat, falling from its peg, stopped, pinned in its downward fall. The knife had caught its brim.

Pablo cursed. It was an expensive hat.

"You kept it from getting dirty, anyhow," he said, grinning.

The laughter which followed that broke off, changed to a roar of welcome. "Silver!" "The bridegroom!" "Up, Hawks! It's the man himself!"

Wide, sloping shoulders, panther-powerful, filled the doorway. Strong, feral white teeth showed in a grin that stretched the mobile, chiseled lips of a generous mouth. Gray eyes, warm and luminous, sparkled above a predatory nose. The man who stood in the doorway was so perfectly proportioned he did not look his size.

Silver Trent. *El Halcon de la Sierra!*

POWER SHOWED in him—vibrated from the easy, great-muscled stance of his body, lay easily, almost lazily, along the lean, glowing lines of his face, laughed out of the depths of his eyes. Power of mind and body beyond other men.

Yet there was more, too. A clear decency, a warmth, some intangible, magnetic thing which changed the careless glances of these hard-bitten men into something close to adoration. Here, it was plain, was a man loved as few men can hope to be. No need for him to declare his leadership by the ordinary claw-and-fang methods of the outlaw wolf pack. The thing was there, clear and pure, not to be questioned.

"*Hola, hijos mios,*" he grinned. "Must you be christening even my wedding day with a gun and a knife?"

"Ay, and with wine of the finest, my little bridegroom!" Doc Brimstone bellowed. "Look—Cerridos! At its best and mellowest."

He pointed to the wine cask.

"Then tap it, Doc," Silver laughed. "Else you'll be bursting like a fermenting keg of wine yourself."

Doc Brimstone shook with laughter, but not long enough to delay the tapping of the keg. When that was done the wine was passed, glass after glass, about the table, while men drank their toasts to Silver Trent.

And if there was a faintly perceptible bitterness in the wine it went unnoticed, or was attributed to an essential quality of a wine older than anyone was in the habit of drinking.

Silver, glass in hand, looked fondly over this gathering of his Hawks. Nowhere on earth, he guessed, could anyone find fighting men to equal them in skill, in ferocity, or in generosity. Outlaws, they profited only when luck sent them a rich man who also seemed evil and unjust. Killers, they killed by no love of killing, but only in ultimate self-defense or when no one could doubt that the killing was needed. Outcasts to the world of respectability, they were friends to every poor devil in need, brothers to every man who plowed a straight furrow and walked the earth in the light of his own courage and conscience.

Silver Trent wondered now how many of them feared in their hearts that he was leaving them. When a man married, things were changed. He acquired other, more important loyalties. His friends no longer came first. Not a bachelor on earth who had not found that out, in some degree or another. Women, even the best of them, played the devil with a good man's life—or changed it for the better, depending on the point of view. But they changed it.

Would it happen to him—Silver? He did not know. He had tried to think that it would not. He was marrying a girl who knew his way of life, and who was ready to live it. She had proven herself, and he knew that she held the respect and affection of these men, not only through her charm and grace, but through her flawless courage.

He would like, he thought, to find some way to say to these, his friends, that he would not change. That he would have the same love for them, the same devoted loyalty. That his courage and his cool audacity would not waver, merely because soft arms waited for him back in the safety of the hideout.

He tried to find words for it, and wondered at himself because his head felt curiously heavy. The thoughts didn't come. Perhaps it was because it was a hard thing to say. Then a queer coldness went into his heart, and he wondered if it wasn't because what he had to say was not true. Perhaps deep inside him he knew that he would change. He remembered the stark fear he had felt the last time Gracia was in danger, how it had almost paralyzed his readiness of action and decision.

The thought made him feel weak and stupid inside. He groped his way to a chair and sat down at the table. This was no time to think, anyway. Maybe he had had too much to drink. But that was funny, too. He had not drunk much. Though he had a tremendous head for liquor, on any occasion, today, his wedding day, he had been unusually careful.

Maybe it was only that his nerves were playing him tricks, he thought. His head felt horribly fuzzy.

Involuntarily, he nodded, put his face on the tablecloth before him. It was absurd, he knew, shameful. He, Silver, couldn't pass out. He had to get himself together.

He became aware that the table was curiously silent, and it stabbed at his pride. They had fallen silent out of embarrassment at seeing their leader too drunk to stay awake. With a violent effort of will, he lifted his head.

Dazedly, he stared. The table was not quiet on account of him. Every man jack of them was drunk! They were lolling back in their chairs, some with heads down on the table. One man was on his feet, staggering. He fell, as Silver watched him. Then it struck him like a bolt between the eyes. Something was wrong! Something was wrong as hell!

Down the board, a great, blond head looked at him out of stunned blue eyes. Lars Johannsen.

17

"I ban dope'," Lars said thickly, unbelievingly, and got to his feet, knocking over his chair and jarring the table so that the dishes rattled.

Dope! Silver knew now. He, too, was doped. It must be the wine. That wine—of—Cerridos. He had to keep awake. Something was hellishly wrong!

He got to his feet, staggering. Lars had gone down to the floor, with a great crash. Now Silver saw a face at the window—a dark face, evil.

ANGER BURNED deep in Silver. It was like fire smothered under layers of stuff that was not inflammable. His anger wanted to burst out, but it couldn't. His will wanted to gather itself up, but something was holding it back. He felt as he had felt once in a dream when he wanted to run, but could not. His weak and rubbery legs made motions, but stayed always, horribly, in the same place.

He got up, and his head whirled, with the sick motion of a dying top. He went down. Falling, his forehead struck the edge of the table.

Dimly, he was aware that the door to the great hall had opened. Footsteps sounded, scuttering.

Frozen-lipped, Silver got to his feet. With an incalculable effort, he pulled himself erect, his hands on the table. Men were in the doorway. As he came up, he saw a knife flash, and heard a choked gasp. The knife had gone into the throat of Juan Beixos, one of the best of his new men. Juan, who had fought with him at the barricades when this very town of Sangre had been attacked. Jaun, who—

18

A flame of anger pierced upward through the cottony stuff that filled Silver's being. He held himself erect with his left hand while his right fumbled for its gun. Sudden flame blasted at him from the end of the table. Afterward, there was a muffled memory of the viciousness of bullets he had heard.

His right hand lifted, heavy—horribly heavy and feeble. Something slapped dully against his palm. The man at the end of the table, with the gun in his hand, coughed, wavered and disappeared from Silver's view. It was as though a fuzzy shadow had flickered out.

Another man stood frozen an endless second, then turned with a panic-stricken cry and plunged for the door. He had a blood-dripping knife in his hand. This was the man who had pierced Juan Beixos throat. Again there was that blow against Silver's palm, and the running man stopped, his back bending backward in a queer jerk. He wavered a moment, then plunged on his face. But the fall of his upper body was disconnected, as though his spine had been snapped in half.

Now at the window, guns were firing, and at the side of the table a blond, leonine head lifted, eyes wavering, uncoordinated—and maddened. Other men were storming in the doorway.

Silver's left gun was out now. He was standing unsupported. But the room was rocking, and the men in the doorway were wavering, snapping about like men in the uncertainty of a desert mirage.

They were hard to hit, bobbing like that, but Silver had shot at moving objects before. He waited until his targets came past the sights of his guns, then let them have it.

Now Lars Johanssen was coming toward him—a great, lurching figure of destruction, with a strained madness in his face. Was Lars going to attack him?

Before the thought was more than a question, he heard a gun bellow behind him. Lars checked in his wild, rolling pace and then went on, cursing thickly. He disappeared behind Silver as the Hawk's guns blasted again, and two of the bobbing, flame-stabbing targets near the door went over.

Another shot sounded behind Silver, and he heard a cursing grunt from Lars, then a strangled cry from another throat and a faint crack that sounded like a man's neck breaking.

A panic-stricken shout sounded—the blast of another gun. Silver frowned. It had begun to seem to him that too many people were firing guns behind his back.

He swung around. Two Mexicans were inside the doorway through which he had entered the room. A third was barely visible behind them. He was barely visible because not only the first two were in the way but Lars' great bulk as well was between them and his leader.

Lars had a hand at each man's neck, and now his great arms swept together. The men's skulls cracked with a popping, crushing sound—like thin ice under a horse's hoofs.

Behind, the third man, his eyes bugging and his face like a sheet, raised a Colt to fire. Silver, his mind and finger moving in the same, difficult stubborn daze, shot him dead.

Then the Hawk turned back to the men at the front door.

One of them was rushing him. He shot as Silver turned. A great white light leaped into Silver's brain, driving out all the effects of the drug, leaving his mind crystal clear for the split second of its glow.

He knew then that he and his men had been drugged so that they might be killed—that these were El Diablo's men—and that only he, Silver, remained to protect everybody from Juan Beixos' fate.

Silver's left gun flashed toward the man who had shot him. It was as though a wind blew the man backward. Silver's right gun stabbed flame and death at another of the figures at the door.

Outside, a sudden roar of voices sounded. One of the men at the door cried a sharp warning. The Hawk's thumb reached for the hammer of his right gun, but somehow it would not get there. That brilliant light had faded. Darkness was seeping in, growing like a black fog. His thumb would not move. He could not see.

Silver fought against it in desperation. He had to see! He couldn't fail his men. He mustn't fail. The thought was like a small circular voice spinning about in the very center of his brain—spinning faster and faster, until it was meaningless.

Then darkness was master, and all things had faded from sight....

CHAPTER 3
START OF THE BLOOD-TRAIL

SILVER FOUGHT his way up through layer after layer of black. He saw anxious faces bent over him, and a babble of voices began. At first he heard their words only in a haze of sound. His memory was struggling to bring him back bits of what had happened.

It came to him finally that this was his wedding day. Then what was he doing sleeping? He sat up abruptly, lurched back as his head rang like the hammers of hell and a sudden overwhelming nausea swept him.

He became aware now that something warm was running down his cheek and that a fiery pain needled his scalp. He put his hand up and found that his head had been bandaged. Memories of the fight began to come back to him. Then the whole thing flashed into his mind. The doped wine. The silent table. The knife in Juan's throat. Lars....

He got to his feet, staggering. Anxious hands reached out to keep him from falling. Voices babbled at him.

His glance swept the table. It was almost as he had seen it last. Only now, the sound of breathing, stentorian and difficult, told him that his men were asleep, unhurt—except where some places were vacant.

"Lars?" he demanded hoarsely. "Lars Johanssen?"

"The doctor has him, *Señor*. He says that he will live."

"Juan? Juan Beixos?"

There was a silence. Then a voice said softly, regretfully. "He is dead, *Señor* Silver. A knife in the throat. The dogs."

There had been something unresolved in the Hawk's mind when he came to, a vague sense of disaster. Now it was a sharp, intolerable sense of grief. Juan—dead! Pain swept him in a weakening flood, then anger, flaming.

He made a sudden gesture of cold acceptance, not knowing how bleak his lean, pallid face had gone, or how the frozen, deadly, unforgiving anger looked out of his eyes.

The sight of it sent the men about him stumbling back from him, as though they almost feared his vengeance on themselves.

The movement brought his consciousness back to him. These men of the town of Sangre were his friends. Once they had followed him into battle.

His eyes softened. "You came to help us, didn't you?" he asked.

"Sí, Señor! Sí!" Their worried voices were a deep expression of loyalty, and Silver did not miss its significance.

"The man who killed Juan is dead," he told them quietly. "But the man who sent the killer is not dead. He will be, one day."

Silver's head felt heavy, still dull, almost bewildered. He wanted to put it down, somewhere. He wanted to rest.

"I will go to the *Señorita Gracia*," he said. "I will—"

He broke off. There was a sudden quality in the silence which got through even to his still-dazed brain.

"Gracia?" he said sharply. "Where is *Señorita Gracia?* Why is she not here?"

The townsmen were silent, their eyes at once frightened and

distressed, and Silver knew the answer to his question before the last words left his lips.

He turned abruptly on the man nearest him. "Well?" he snapped. "Answer!"

The man stammered. "They—they took her, *Señor*. They—"

Silver had him by the throat, his great gray eyes blazing, suddenly insane. "You lie, you dog!" he stormed. "By God—"

The man goggled at him, his face draining of color, while another hand plucked at Silver's sleeve.

"It was the first thing they did, *Señor*," the second man said pleadingly. "Even before they came to kill you, they took the *señorita* and the *padre*. We did not know. There was the sexton there. They cracked his skull, but he was able to tell us afterward what had happened. And others saw them riding out of town—half a dozen armed men, with the *señorita* and the *padre* in their midst. Meanwhile, there was the firing here. And we ran to help you—"

Silver released his savage grip on the first man's throat. "I am sorry, friend," he said. "I—I'm sorry...."

The townsman made a little, almost apologetic gesture with his hand. *"De nada, Señor,"* he gasped. "It is nothing."

SILVER LIFTED his head and turned his gaze around the group which filled the room. "Thank you," he said heavily. "Thank you all, my friends." Then he turned and walked out of the room.

His walk was slow, stumbling, because the drug was still working in him, and because of the shock of the news.

He found old Juan—who was no kin to the Juan who had

died but who was Padre Pete's servant—weeping in the Padre's quarters.

"I was in the kitchen, *Señor*," he began tearfully.

Silver cut him off. "Which way did they go, Juan?"

"It is said to the southwest, *Señor*. I think—"

"Get me coffee—strong and black."

To the southwest, of course, Silver knew. They would not bother trying to deceive anyone. In the great, deep strip of the badlands to the southwest, they could find safety enough. And then beyond it were range on range of bleak and arid mountains for concealment.

Anywhere in a whole quarter of the far horizon! The nearer country Silver and his men knew well. El Diablo, after his great defeat, had not ventured there.

Some place far off. And what would happen to Gracia meanwhile? Silver dared not think of that. The present task was hard enough. He must keep his emotions out of it. If he was to find her, he needed all the clarity of his brain, all the cool cunning and determination of which he was capable.

The coffee helped to clear his head. He drank great cupfuls of it, strong and black, and then ordered his horse.

The sunlight had gone when he started, blotted out by a great black cloud. There were two men who might have recognized that cloud—might have told that it once bore the shape of a cask of wine, and then of a death's head. But their tongues were silent forever.

Silver rode through crowded, silent streets, while the beginnings of thunder muttered in the cloud to the southwest, and a swift wind whipped the dust up into his face.

The fiesta crowds were voiceless as he passed. But hats came off in silence, as though men greeted a funeral cortège.

Once he was past, the mutter arose, like an undertone to the growing thunder. "I would not like to be El Diablo now." "If I had those eyes to face, *compadre,* I would not dare hide behind the fires of Hell itself." "Do you remember how he came into this town when all were against him and—" "Hush, hombre! He is more than human, our Hawk, but the Devil also is less than human.... Who are we to say—?"

Then the lightning flashed out of the dark depths of the cloud—a bolt in Silver's path, so close that his horse reared wildly and sought to turn. The rain came, in a gust of fury.

A townswoman, peering from the window of an adobe shack near the edge of Sangre, crossed herself. "It is a sign," she breathed. "He should not go on."

"It's not the lightning that will stop him," her husband growled, "nor the fires of Hell either," he added under his breath.

The woman looked at him severely. "I believe you'd like to ride with him, Imbecile."

"Por Dios," the man breathed. "If he would but nod his head to me…!"

The woman still stared, but the expression of her eyes suddenly softened. "I am married to a fool," she murmured, "but also to a man."

SILVER TRENT had no room in his heart for anything but

a curse for the rain, which washed out all tracks, all sign. The devil's luck was with the devil, it seemed.

After that came days which the Hawk scarcely remembered. Days with the barren, contorted battlements of the malpai leering at him, with the glass-sharp rock of the slopes reaching for his horse's hoofs. Days from dawn to dark in the saddle, half fed, unwatered, the animal under him gaunted and heavy-hoofed with exhaustion.

All this time he could find no sign—no trace of the girl, who, he knew now, was the very breath of life itself to him.

Then, one day at evening, there was a fleck of fire against the dusk, and Silver rode in on the camp of an ancient Mexican who eked out a meager living from the sale of the armadillo shells he hunted.

Gravely, courteously, he offered the facilities of his poor camp to the gaunt, fever-eyed *caballero*.

"Have you seen men who rode with a girl or a priest?" Silver asked the automatic question wearily, expecting the universal negative.

"*Sí, Señor,*" the old Mexican answered. "I have seen. There were seven who rode with a *señorita* and a *padre*—the latter having their hands bound behind them. I concealed myself, not knowing what temper they might show. For I have lived long by minding my own affairs."

He peered at Silver out of rheumy eyes, which nevertheless had the desert rat's appearance of gazing into far distances.

"Yet you *Señor*—there is that about you—I do not know what.

It is as though there were something to which I might trust my poor life itself."

"And you do not know me, *viejo?*" Silver asked gently.

"I have not seen you before, my son," the old man answered wonderingly, "yet it is as though I had known you always."

Silver had a crooked smile for him. "At least we have met now," he said. "It may be that your last days will not be the worse for it. Shall we sleep?"

In the morning, he wrote briefly on a piece of paper and drew a handful of silver from his pocket.

"Will you take this to the town of Sangre for me?" he asked quietly. "Give it to any man who will say that he is a man of the Hawk."

The ancient stared at him. "Do you mean you are of the Hawks?" he demanded breathlessly. "You are—"

"I am what I am," Silver said. "Will you take my message for me?"

"Not in a year will I see so much money," the old man quavered, "yet if you are a man of *El Halcon,* put it back in your pocket. Is there a poor man in this land who would not serve such as he gladly?"

Silver tossed the money into his lap. "Yet take it," he said. "And if the message finds its mark, it may be that you will not be poor for the rest of your days."

He climbed into the saddle, and suddenly there was no fatigue left in him. He had found the trail he sought. And it seemed almost as though his mount understood that the hopelessness of the search was over, for the stallion tossed his head and stepped out bravely.

"You'll have rest soon, pardner," Silver told him. "It won't be safe to ride you long."

TWO DAYS later, a man trudged into the huddle of a Mexican village high in the middle of the badlands. It was a queer, an almost astonishing phenomenon, this village, for it should not have been there at all. It was a freak of nature, created by virtue of the fact that the earth had designed to yield water here, and permit, in the midst of desolation, something like a wide oasis where men might graze goats and even farm.

The man, actually, was almost as astonishing as the village. Or so, apparently, thought the villager who ran from what passed for an inn among that huddle of adobe shacks. He stared, open-mouthed, at the stranger.

"I seek a place to stay the night, brother," the newcomer said, in fluent peon dialect.

He was a big man—too big, almost, for a Mexican. He was dressed in a pair of ragged cotton pants, a shirt which had seen better days, and a tall, straw sombrero. His skin, face, hands and feet, which were bare, were Indian-brown. He drove a burro before him and carried a guitar on his back.

"*Dios!*" the innkeeper muttered to himself. "A minstrel, and in this country! Truly, these days bring me strange sights."

"What do you say?" Eyes, gray-black, held him steadily.

"I say you are welcome, *hombre*," the innkeeper answered hastily. "Enter my poor house, which is yours."

He turned, and Silver followed him, something like a smile

shadowing his lips. This disguise of his, he saw, did poorly even in this light of sunset. Yet it was the best he had been able to improvise at the hut of the goatherd he had found at the edge of the hills that surrounded this valley. It would, he knew, go better in a more populous countryside, and better still at night, when the gray of his eyes did not show so well. But it was better to be disguised even a little than to ride into El Diablo's country alone and as his proper self.

Silver knew that he ought to have waited for his message to reach his men, but he had wasted so much time casting here and there in an effort to pick up the trail that he dared not lose another day.

Had he taken time to think, he would, he knew, have been here, in this place, earlier. Anyone who really knew this country could have guessed at the trail and been nearly certain of being right. But he had been half-maddened at the thought of what might be happening to Gracia at any moment, and he had not gone about it with such cold logic. He had tried, single-handed, all the possibilities in this barren land, and as each possibility had failed, he had cursed himself for his blind blundering.

He followed the innkeeper into the three-room adobe shack with the jaunty air which he assumed as part of his disguise. But there was no muscle or nerve in all his big, mountain-cat body that was not shrilling protest against the abuse to which it had been subjected. Silver knew that the utter weariness which possessed him was as much nervous and emotional as it was physical. Without the strain of thinking of what might have happened to Gracia and the driving need to get to her, his body might have taken even such a beating as he had given it without coming so close to utter exhaustion.

HE WAS almost too tired to eat the red beans bathed in chili and the goat's milk cheese which the innkeeper set before him. He forced himself to it, knowing that he must not trust himself long to the stimulation of the raw *tequila* which was the only drink this hostelry had to offer.

The innkeeper, a goat-herd who made a little extra money by virtue of owning a three-room house, sat opposite him as he ate, and Silver was careful to talk to him as a friend and an equal.

At the end of the meal, he had pushed aside his plate, grinning, and murmured, *"Bueno!"* Not until now did he trust himself to ask the question which had all along been on his lips.

"By chance, have my friends with the *señorita* passed by here?"

Justin, the inkeeper, looked honestly surprised. "There has been no *señorita, amigo,*" he said slowly. "Some men came one morning a week ago, commanded food and drink of me, and took it with them, riding off without paying—may the Devil take them and their wives and children! Three of them. There were others waiting, but I saw them only from afar. Since then, I have had other guests—one, a man such as is not often seen."

"Yes?" Silver said encouragingly.

The hillman narrowed his eyes. *"Amigo,"* he said, "you are sympathetic, therefore I tell you. He was a great bull of a man—a gringo. Yellow of hair, with eyes like a puma of the mountains. He asked after a big man—one, he said, almost as big as himself—with the nose of a hawk and eyes which might be the color of a winter lake or like a gray cloud with the sun shining through it. But I had not then seen such a man, and I told him so."

Silver caught his breath suddenly, sharply. He leaned forward, drilling this Mexican with his gaze. "Go on," he said sharply. "What happened? Tell me what this man was like."

The innkeeper described his guest in such detail that there could be no doubt of his identity. Such a description could only apply to Lars Johanssen!

Yet that was not possible. Or was it…?

Silver laughed softly to himself. Yes, it was possible. Where he had had to follow all trails himself, his men could have split, and divided the work. He had been a fool of fools not to wait for them. He could see them suddenly back there, waking up to find what their drinking had cost him. It would not be likely that they would all remain idle. And while he had been casting about, Lars had taken that part of the sector assigned to him and pushed ahead.

"Two days, you say?" Silver questioned the innkeeper swiftly. "He stayed the night? Which way did he go in the morning?"

"I can't answer your questions, friend."

Silver looked at him. "Why?" he asked, his voice ominous.

The hillman drew a sudden breath and his face lost color. "You are he, then, certainly," he breathed. "But when he said eyes like a winter lake, I knew not that he meant a frozen lake of Hell!"

"Talk to the point. Where did he go?"

"He meant to stay the night," the innkeeper said quickly. "If he did or not, I do not know. All I know is that when I went to call him in the morning, he was not there. And there was blood on his bed!"

CHAPTER 4
THE SHADOW ON THE WALL

SILVER'S HAND licked out across the table with the speed of a snake striking. His fingers gripped the innkeeper's shirt below the chin. *"Hombre,"* he said, savage-eyed. "I am a friend to my friends, but I think that ill luck will follow you if you try to double-cross me. What do you know of what happened to this man?"

The Mexican's thick lips were suddenly dry, his voice babbling.

"How should I know, *Señor?"* he stammered. "I—I— Listen to me, *Señor.* There is a house—a *casita*—yellow like the color of the land. If you go there...."

"Where is it?"

"Two miles along the road, *Señor.* To the southwest. If the *Señor* will go aside from the trail a little—by the bridge over Lizard Canyon—in the morning, playing his guitar...."

"Why? Why then?"

"Because two men we do not know are staying there. Perhaps...."

Silver let go his grip suddenly. He could not have said exactly why he was so certain that this man was lying to him. He had suspected it before, and that had been the reason for his pretended anger, his sudden grip on the man's shirt. It hadn't

33

been to shake the truth out of him, but to put enough fear in him to spoil his act, to bring the lie into his scared eyes.

"*Bueno!*" the Hawk said, suddenly quiet, "tomorrow we will see whether or not you are imagining things. My friend was wounded. It may be he bled a little in his sleep. But," here he looked sullen and ominous, "tomorrow I will have a look at these two strangers of yours."

He reached out and poured himself another drink of *tequila*, then filled a glass for the innkeeper. "Here's thanks to you for your friendship, friend," he said. "I need it. I am very tired, and I can use whatever help good men will give me."

He drank and then yawned sleepily. There was no difficulty about that. He was desperately weary, desperately in need of sleep in a bed.

On impulse, it appeared, the innkeeper leaned forward and said, "Two other men came through, *Señor*, after that first gringo. They were *Mexicanos* these—a thin man who spoke of the saints, and another, one whose race I could not determine, yet he was an *etranjero*—one with a wooden leg. They stayed one night, and then went on."

This time, Silver betrayed no trace of surprise or emotion. He was on guard now, but his heart was pumping suddenly, violently. Pablo? At any rate, Big Nose Beaujolais, for a certainty. Oh, yes, they had not been idle, his men! Three of them had struck the trail!

Nor, it appeared, had El Diablo been idle. He had bought this innkeeper, unless Silver's instincts were all wrong. For an instant he considered trying to outbid the buyer, but that would mean tipping his own hand. He decided against it.

He yawned again, pretending to care nothing about the peglegged man and his companion. After a little, he asked to be shown his sleeping quarters.

The innkeeper showed him to a room on the ground floor. There was one window through which came a mixed stench of pigpen and goats. Silver turned out the lamp and lay down on the thin pallet which served as a bed.

For minutes he lay there, fighting sleep in a desperate and losing battle. After a while, because the struggle was too much for him, he got up and knelt by his cot, in the most uncomfortable position he could devise, and pretended to snore. At times, the pretense became a reality, so that he nodded and almost fell on his face.

He wished desperately, as the minutes and the hours passed, that he had knocked his host on the head and gone his way— though what he would have done with the man's wife and daughter he did not know.

Once, he heard soft footsteps outside the door of his room. Then, whoever it was, went away, the sound of his walking showing less care. He guessed that it was the innkeeper, come to see if he was really asleep.

He waited an endless time after that, then got to his feet. He staggered on paralyzed knees to the window, and slid out of it. The night was dark. Only star-glimmer showed the way.

SILVER CIRCLED and took the road to the southwest.

It was not that he guessed it was not safe to sleep in his bed.

Rather it was because he had a hunch that the time for him to get to that house by the bridge was when he was not expected.

He moved along the side of the road, walking softly and

Silver felt an instinctive
ripple of warning at his back.

slowly. After awhile, he heard what he had been listening for—
the footsteps of a man walking toward the inn.

He slid off the side of the road, found a clump of greasewood
and lay behind it. The footsteps came on, walking quietly but
briskly. A moment later, a form loomed through the darkness—
the heavy, short-legged, unmistakable form of the innkeeper.

Silver held his breath as the man passed within a few feet of
him. When he had disappeared, he got to his feet silently and

followed. It was as he had suspected. A trap had been laid for him. He would be expected to go to that house by the bridge tomorrow. And he would never reach there alive.

He smiled grimly in the darkness and went on, cat-silent on his bare feet.

Sleep and fatigue alike had fled out of him. His nerves were tense, his every faculty alert. The messages of his senses came to him so fast and so multitudinously that his mind had difficulty in sorting them out. The varying feel of the night air on his skin; the thousand separate odors that his nostrils quivered to; the infinite, minute sounds that registered in exquisite confusion on his ears; the shapes, the forms, the shadows that his cat-eyes picked out in the darkness—all these made a bewildering pattern of subtly graded perceptions for his mind to classify and judge. Though on more than one occasion his supernormal sensitiveness had preserved his life, sometimes he was tempted to think it was a handicap.

Even the clarity of his night vision was in some sort a disadvantage, for he could never believe that a shadow could quite conceal him from ordinary eyes. To him the night was not black but gray. There were even colors in it—deep blues and purples and faint lavenders, as well as silver and black and all the shades between, and the yellow glint of starlight like a luminescence in the air.

Experience had taught him that few other men could see as he could in the dark, but it was hard for him to understand. And now, as so often, there was a sudden wistfulness on him because he must always see things only in terms of danger. He would have given much to be able to walk through this scented and speaking darkness with his senses attuned only to its infinite fascination and beauty. But there was no chance of that. His existence depended too much on an ever-vigilant guard against peril.

Yet because there was little fear in Silver Trent, there was a kind of keyed up pleasure in him, too. It was only that he regretted that this pleasure was not pure, as he would have liked it to be.

Ahead of him in the road, a gray-dark rope moved and coiled. Silver smiled. It was a big snake for this high country. The soft, strong muskiness of it had come to his nostrils even before he had seen it, and his eyes had taken it in even before it coiled.

For an instant, he hesitated, wanting to pass it by. There was deep in him a kinship for everything savage and deadly. But he remembered that there were children around here. Regretfully, he held his course toward it until the dry chill vibration of the rattle sang its quick, hair-lifting song. Half a dozen feet from it he stopped, eyes fixed on the swaying, threatening head. Then his body swayed toward the snake in a movement equally threatening, and swayed backward as the reptile struck.

The strike fell short of his bare foot by six inches, so that the flat, vicious triangular head thudded on the dust of the roadway. Silver's hand moved like another snake striking. It caught the diamondback just behind the head and his fingers twisted, snapping the backbone. An instant later his other hand caught the writhing body behind, and his hands snapped apart. The snake's flesh parted, and Silver tossed the two sections to the side of the road and went on.

WHEN HE estimated that he had come about a mile and a half, he left the road, paralleling it in the grass and sagebrush of the rising ground on either side. He slid, shadow-silent through the brush until a yellow gleam of lamplight showed ahead. The sight of it surprised him. He had not expected anybody to be awake at this hour.

Presently, a faint murmur of voices came to him from the right. He went toward them, his bare feet making little whispery silken sounds in the dust and grass—sounds which would have scarcely been audible to any other ears, even so close. But to him they sounded loud, as did the rub of his clothing and the sharp, rhythmic thunder of his pulses.

Then, ahead, he could make out two forms. He slid toward them, under cover of the sage. Low, contemptuous laughter came to his ears…. "Pretending to snore on his knees," a voice said in Spanish. "That's a good one!"

Silver stopped short, feeling a hot flood of humiliation and anger stain his cheeks. So the innkeeper had been able to get a look at him. Had made a fool of him!

"Keep quiet, will you?" another voice hissed. "You may think this fellow is easy, but he ain't. Pancho said he thought it was Silver Trent himself. An' he's liable to be along here any minute."

"Dios! Stop the trembling of your knees, *amigo.* I can see the road a quarter of a mile away. If he comes, he will die—Hawk or not. He has ears no longer than another's!"

Silver's lips flattened. Slowly, silently, he moved forward.

The wrangling subdued voices continued, but even silence would not have let them hear his ghostly approach. He could see their backs now plainly, as they sat watching the lighter ribbon of the road, expecting to catch, in the starlight, any moving shadow on it.

Narrow-eyed, he crept forward, until they were no more than two yards in front of him. If either turned his head, Silver would be in plain view. For a moment, he hesitated. He had only to level the gun in his hand and murmur to them to be silent, now. But there was the off-chance that one would try something, make some move that would force him to shoot, and that would alarm the others. For Silver had no belief whatever in the innkeeper's statement that there were only two men here. And he guessed that not only his life, but Lars', and maybe Pablo's and Big Nose's, depended on how he handled this situation.

So he moved forward again, unbreathing, slow, and infinitely silent. He was within three feet of the pair before they sensed his presence. Suddenly, one of them stiffened. He started to turn—as though his very backbone had felt the creeping threat behind it.

Silver did not wait. His right hand lashed out and laid the barrel of his gun behind the man's ear. The crunch of steel on mastoid bone sounded loud in the dark silence.

The other man whipped about, a hoarse cry breaking from his lips. The gun barrel smashed along his jawbone. This time, the sound of steel on bone was accompanied by a crack as the man's jaw broke. He dropped, groaning faintly.

TIGHT-LIPPED, SILVER stopped the groaning, by

41

clipping him behind the ear. Then he turned, listening, as a startled exclamation sounded above, from the direction of the lighted cabin.

He glided swiftly behind a bush. Footsteps sounded, running toward the men he had knocked out.

"Luiz! Antonio!" a hushed voice called.

"Dios! What has happened?"

Silver stepped into the open as two figures passed him and bent over the recumbent figures of their companions.

"Don't make any noise, friends," he said softly. "I would not like to shoot your backbones out. Put your hands in the air."

They froze, as though suddenly paralyzed. Slowly, their arms went above their heads.

"Do not turn around," Silver instructed them. "Stand so—just as you are. Where are the others?"

The man on the right spoke quickly. "There are no others, *Señor*. You have us all. I beg you, spare us. We have done no harm."

Silver thought a moment. The man—perhaps because of the crawling fear in his voice—sounded as though he were telling the truth. Because of that, Silver hated to use the barrel of his gun again. But he had neither rope nor anything to make a gag—and he could not risk believing a man of El Diablo's.

El Diablo. The very thought of the name hardened Silver's heart. The coyotes who took his pay were not deserving of much consideration.

"My friends?" he questioned softly. "The big blond man and the others—where are they?"

"In the cabin, *Señor,*" the quavering-voiced speaker answered him. "We have not harmed them. We were but guarding them."

"I hope for your sake that you have not harmed them," Silver's grim murmur sounded. Then his gun barrel flicked twice, with a speed so great that the second man had not even a moment in which to try to duck before the steel caught him. He dropped, hitting the ground only a split second later than his companion.

Silver disarmed all four, tossing their guns into the brush. Then he turned toward the cabin. The light still burned there, though the place was utterly silent. He wondered whether or not the man he had just slugged had told the truth.

Warily, cat-footed, he approached the door. It opened to his touch, and he stepped into the lamplit room. Then his breath went out of him in a sigh of relief. They were all there.

Bound, their eyes flamed at him in welcome and in warning. He stepped toward Pablo, intending to cut his bonds swiftly and then move toward the other two, Lars and the beefy, muscular form of Big Nose Beaujolais.

As he unsheathed a knife to cut Pablo's bound arms, Silver felt again that instinctive ripple of warning at his back. His eye caught the sinister, rifle-holding shadow on the wall. He flashed sideways and down.

Rifle lead hurtled past him. In the same split second a sixgun hammered the silent air of the hut into a hell of yelling sound.

CHAPTER 5
THE SECRET HILLS

F LAT ON the floor, rolling, Silver whipped his gun up and slammed lead into the forward-leaning body of the rifleman. The Mexican broke in the middle, slid forward on his face.

Behind him, the sixgun blared again, but even as he shot, the gunman was jerking backward toward the safety of the dark, and his bullet missed, howling past Silver's ear to bury itself in the adobe of the floor.

Silver snapped a shot at the disappearing figure, but knew, as the hammer fell, that he had shot too late. Running footsteps beat outside, and he whipped to his feet, racing toward the door.

The footsteps sounded now around the corner of the house. Silver rushed after them, turned the corner to see a dim figure hurtling through the brush. He snapped a shot at it but missed, then ran on. But the noise of his own running spoiled his hearing and he stopped. When he had located the other again, a new sound had been added—the sound of a horse's stamping hoofs. Then the horse's hoofs were a sudden thunder in the night.

Silver stopped, cursing softly. One man, at least, had gotten away. And that was enough to warn El Diablo of what had happened.

For a moment, he hesitated, thinking that he ought to find a mount and run this man down, but he was still uncertain of how many guards there were here. And there were his own men to think of. When he got back to the cabin, Pablo had already undone the bonds of the others.

44

"How many were there, Pablo?" Silver snapped.

"Six only," the lean and pious one answered. "How many did you get?"

"Five," Silver answered, for the moment disconsolate, "one of them got away."

"Dot ban not'in," Lars Johannsen put in, getting to his feet. "Won man went out before. Dey know already dot we are here."

The fact—the precious and almost unbelievable fact that they *were* here—swept over Silver anew.

"How did it happen that you came?" he asked softly, "and where are the rest of the boys?"

Pablo gestured. "We divided it up," he said. "We knew their camp must be somewhere in this quarter—to the southwest. There wasn't any other place Varro—El Diablo—could be hiding out. But it was a lot of country to get through. We split, and divided the work. But we decided we'd meet at a town up here in the mountains, about fifty miles from here—San Gabriel de la Sierra. That way, we'd be able to team up again."

Silver drew a long breath. "I reckon I lost my head some," he said soberly. "I should have waited on you boys." Then he smiled. "But I sent word back to you," he added by way of extenuation. "I reckon it won't reach anybody now, because I sent it to Sangre."

Big Nose Beaujolais grinned. "Wrong again, Chief," he said cheerfully. "Beau Buchanan and a few of the others stayed on, just in case you'd do that very thing!"

Silver's face colored, then he grinned. "I give up," he said softly. "You've out-thought me all the way through."

Pablo smiled grimly. "Not exactly. Working alone, you got

onto the trail that we lucked into because this part of the country was assigned to us. And working alone, you got us out of the jam that our own dumbness got us into. They were only holding us alive until they could get their hands on you. Then they were going to kill us and take you in to Varro, to be tortured and killed at his pleasure."

Silver's jaw tightened. "Speaking of them," he said, "I don't know just how hard I tapped them. We'd better see—before they wake up. Then maybe we can get a little talk out of them."

AS IT turned out, they did get a good deal of talk out of their prisoners. Threatened, they told all they knew, which was a lot and not much. Esteban Varro's country, they said, lay beyond the Iron Mountains—*las Montañas Hierras*—and except for one secret trail there was no way to get to it other than a detour of hundreds of miles.

"And the secret trail?" Pablo said, his lean fanatic features suddenly cruel, ruthless. "Speak quickly, little friend, so that I will not have to build a fire on your breastbone."

The man who had quavered in his talk while Silver listened in the dark, stammered and sputtered now in terror. *"Señor,* we do not know! Believe me. We are not of El Diablo's men. Never, has any man told us the secret of this trail—"

"Be silent," Pablo commanded, his voice soft and wholly sinister. "I do not wish to listen to any lies. Anyway, I have wanted to see the good flame burn into your flesh, eating toward the carrion you call your heart, ever since my eyes have sickened at the sight of your dog's face. Lars, put him down."

"Señor! Señor!" the man's voice was a squawl of terror. "I swear

to you. We are but simple men. We have had to be bandits, else we starve in this barren land. But of El Diablo we know nothing beyond his name and the money one brought us, buying our services. *Madre de Dios!* I beg you—"

"Enough, Pablo," Silver said curtly. "This fool is too frightened to lie. But tell me, *hombre,* and be careful of your tongue—what is this talk of a land of El Diablo's? Once, he was supposed to have a land, below there, toward the valley lands about Sangre. But this he has no longer. What mean you by your talk of a land beyond the mountains?"

THE MEXICAN stared at him agape. "I know nothing of this—this land of the valley, *Señor,*" he said. "Always, while we could remember, there were tales of the power of one called Esteban Varro, the Devil, who held the land beyond the mountains, and whom no man dared to disobey. Have you not heard of the Mines of Hell?"

"The Mines of Hell?" Silver repeated slowly. His frozen gray gaze drove into the eyes of the Mexican like a steel drill. "Do you mean that you have known of Esteban Varro long, and that it is he who operates these mines?"

"But, *Señor!*" the man gasped. "You have not heard of him? Why, he is lord of all that land. Even to whisper his name with disrespect is to die. For telling you this, I also shall surely find a knife in my throat unless my good horse can carry me far enough."

"And yet you tell?"

"*Señor,* what am I to do but choose the farthest death. I have looked on the face of this *caballero* who calls always on the names of the saints, and I have drowned myself in the frozen death of your eyes—you who walk without sound in the night. Better to die even tomorrow than today. What I tell you is truth, as God watches me."

"And you have not heard of this man in the country below?"

"We hear nothing of the country below, *Señor*, except of the Great Hawk of the Sierras, whom none has seen. The innkeeper told us that you were surely he, *Señor*, and I believed it until the light shone on you and now I know him for a liar. For the Purple Caul of Murder is not on you. That is to be seen. And besides, he who is the Hawk would have dipped his beak in the blood of my throat long ere this!"

Pablo's sudden, deadly snarl brought a gray whiteness in the captive's face, more deathlike than his former frightened pallor.

"Do you dare blaspheme in the name of the Hawk, worm of a man?"

The Mexican shrank from him in terror. *"Señor!"* he gasped. "Your pardon! I meant—"

"Nothing!" Silver said crisply. "Let him be, Pablo. The Hawk, friend, is not such as you think—for I am he. Go now. You and your *compadres* are free. But go to the north and the east, and do not take again the money of hell."

The Mexican looked at him with jaw dropped and eyes bulging. "You?" he breathed. "You, the Hawk? But…!"

"But nothing," Silver said gently. "Go! In time, you may learn many things."

They went, all four of them, while Pablo looked at Silver out of reproachful eyes. Silver smiled and put a hand on his shoulder.

"They did not harm you, old friend," he said. "Let them go. I am sure now that they are ignorant men, dupes of El Diablo."

YET THAT evening, and the next day, while he held them there, Silver was thoughtful. He had been a fool, he saw, to have believed that El Diablo's power in the valley lands in the past had rested only on the wealth of his ranch there. He should have known that even such a ranch as that would not have provided Esteban Varro with the power and corruption he wielded.

He had been blinded, for one thing, by the fact that Varro had robbed a bullion train just before he had started his revolution. But the fruits of that robbery had not been more than twenty thousand dollars. How could he, Silver, have believed that such a sum could have financed the arms, ammunition and supplies for nearly five thousand men? He had been blind, and worse than blind. For he had believed that in crushing Varro's army and looting his hacienda he had broken the man's power entirely.

He saw now that this kidnapping of his bride was more than a mere revenge of a defeated enemy. It was the cunning move of a man who was still so powerful that he wished nothing so much as to lure Silver and his men into the territory where he yet reigned as king. He had planned to kill Silver, and his Hawks with him, there in Sangre, but if that failed, he wished nothing better than to be followed into the mountains, where he could hold Gracia as bait, until his enemy blundered innocently into his hands.

Silver knew El Diablo as only men know others when they have shared the long intimacy of hatred—and he understood suddenly that the quest he had now undertaken came close to

49

being suicide. If Esteban Varro had planned this, then it was because he had all confidence in his own power, because all the cards were stacked in his favor. And Gracia—Gracia was in his hands!

It was the one thought that Silver could not face wholly. It ripped along his nerves and heart, put a blindness of helpless rage into his mind so that he could hardly think with any sanity at all. He knew that Esteban Varro must have counted on that also!

By sheer will power he held himself in, and waited. By some miracle of self-control he let the days pass, until at last those of his men who had stayed in Sangre rode up. His message had reached there!

A long gust of breath went out of Silver. He had been on the verge of going off without them, of going to the town ahead where the rest of his men had agreed to gather. He had, in fact, been on the verge of going screaming crazy at the thought of what might be happening to Gracia, but, iron-willed, he had held back. Gracia had already been a week in Varro's hands, and it would be a week more, at the least, before he could come up with her. So, in the cold light of common sense, *there was no hurry.* That was what his mind told him, but his emotions went mad inside him.

Then, five minutes after he had looked into the smiling eyes of Beau Buchanan and the four men with him, they were on their way.

A DAY later, they rode weary mounts into the town of San

Gabriel de la Sierra. Nine of them now, riding grim-faced into that small mountain village.

It appeared strangely quiet, subdued. No one was on the streets, and the eyes that peered out at them from the houses were furtive and frightened. Silver's jaw tightened. He began to regret that he had not reconnoitered more fully. Anything might happen here.

Then, from the end of the street, a sudden, ululating blood-curdling yell broke out, and for the first time in many days Silver laughed in pure pleasure. For that figure dancing there in the street was Magpie Myers, and out of the cantina before which he stood other figures were boiling, yelling. And these were his men, too.

Silver laughed to Beau and Pablo, who rode at his side, and set spurs to his horse.

It was a reunion which brought the inhabitants of San Gabriel out of their houses, bug-eyed, as some two score swaggerers clapped one another on the shoulders and stormed the cantina for *tequila* to celebrate their coming together.

They were all there—Pablo and Beau and Lars and Big Nose Beaujolais, with the men who had ridden with Beau, and Ricardo and Miguel and Doc Brimstone and Magpie and Jim Clane and Leon Costillo and Gomez of the scarred face, and Basilio, the hunchback, and half a dozen others, who would have been famous in their own right had they not chosen to ride with men who were so outstanding. The men of the Hawk—who looked into one another's eyes like brothers.

Watching them, Silver's heart swelled as it always did at this sight. Then he remembered Juan—Juan, who would never ride with them again, and his face turned bleak and unforgiving.

He shook the memory off. Some day El Diablo would pay this score also, along with the other debts he owed to Silver Trent.

"The town looks scared," he said to Magpie. "What's happened?"

The oldster laughed. "They ain't quite sure of us yet," he said. "There was some of Varro's crowd waitin' to ambush us when we fust come in. It was only luck that I smelled 'em before they got in any good licks. We run 'em out, countin' coup on four of 'em. Miguel got a leg-scratch out of it, and Leon a bullet through the upper arm. We got purty tough with the town after that, jest to be sure. But they didn't have nothin' to do with it. It was just a question, on their part, of layin' low for both outfits an' not carin' much who won."

Silver found that Magpie also had heard of the secret trail through the mountains, but had been unable to find anybody who knew of it. "Hell! it's just talk, I reckon," he said.

"If there's no secret one, we'll find a public one," Silver said grimly.

Magpie pulled at his yellow-stained white mustache. "I ain't sayin' no," he answered quietly. "In fact, I'm sayin' yes. But have you had a look at them mountains?"

Silver's eyes flicked toward him, suddenly alert. When Magpie talked like this, it was worthwhile paying attention.

"I had a glance at them comin' in," he said. "They didn't look so good, though I saw 'em far off."

Magpie took his arm. "Come an' have another look," he said grimly.

SILVER WENT with him into the street and walked to the end of it. San Gabriel stood on a ridge between two valleys. One, he and his men had just crossed. The other lay before him. Beyond it was the iron rampart of the mountains.

The valley rose sharply on the other side to rimrock that lifted a thousand unrelenting feet and ran left and right as far as the eye could see. Back of that, the ranges of the mountains reared, stark and almost treeless, their metal-colored flanks rising tier on tier to where the high peaks showed snow-covered, remote and forbidding in the late afternoon light.

Silver stared at it a long time, silent, his eyes searching vainly for some flaw, some weakness in that rocky armor. His face grew momentarily more bleak and strained.

"This place where El Diablo is supposed to run things is beyond the far range, accordin' to the talk," Magpie said soberly.

Silver said nothing. There was a weight under his breastbone that felt like lead.

"And this passageway," he said after a moment, tight-throated.

"Ain't to be found," Magpie growled. "The talk is that, a man could spend a year an' not find it."

"Then we'll have to go the hard way," Silver said, his eyes suddenly unrelenting.

"Yeah," Magpie answered steadily, and then added, "No horses, I reckon."

"Hell," Silver said with a wry grin, "I'd say not even mountain goats could make it."

Magpie had a dry laugh for that. "Well, we ain't goats," he said. "We ought to get by."

Silver turned a sudden glance on him. "The men?" he asked, and there was the shadow of a doubt in his voice.

These men of his were riders. If they wanted to go from one saloon to another, a hundred yards up the street, they climbed into the saddle. Walking was a thing they had never practiced.

Magpie chuckled with the corners of his mouth turned down.

"They'll go where you lead 'em," he grunted. "It's time they learned to use their feet for somethin' besides puttin' 'em up on tables anyway!"

The sun slid down the sky and dipped suddenly behind the far, snow-capped peaks. Long shadows ran out from the rimrock, reaching across the valley. The colors of the ranges—metallic orange and red and steel brown—faded to blue, to gray slate, to cold black. The sun set off hidden fireworks behind the peaks. Great streamers of scarlet and gold and bloody purple shot up into the sky. They faded, and the colors of the far hills deepened.

A chill settled on the air. The dimming bulk of the mountains seemed suddenly infinitely remote and forbidding. A profound silence and a hostile, cold drabness lay like a mantle upon them.

Silver drew a long breath. "God help us then," he said soberly, "for the Devil never will."

CHAPTER 6
AT BAY

THEY RODE across the valley, taking with them some natives of the town to lead the horses back. For it was obvious that they would have to leave them there. Then Magpie yelled, "Saw off your boot-heels, you bat-eared, ridin' sons! From now out, I'm gonna teach you what yore maw ought to have taught you long ago."

Climbing from their mounts, they were soon all whittling at the high heels of their riding boots, listening with pleasure while Ricardo of the swagger and the dancing eyes launched into a detailed recountal of Magpie's doubtful ancestry—a swift and biting summary which might have made a poet look to his imagination and most surely would have brought a blush to the cheek of a mule. But it appeared to make no impression on Magpie at all. "Me havin' been cussed by experts," as he explained blandly.

They were all grinning when Silver got to his feet, jaunting the eighty pound pack on his shoulders as though it were a sack of Durham.

"Let's go, hellions," he said cheerfully. "I'm giving a dollar bonus to the first man that strikes gold!"

And that way they began their climb up the rimrock, and entered laughing on a trek which was to prove more than any man could be asked to stand.

The first night out found them with unaccustomed muscles shrilling protest. But the grin was still on their faces when camp was made. Ten days later showed them hardened, lean, and

Doc Brimstone   Gracia   Magpie Meyers

beginning to be grim. Hunger was gnawing under their tightened belt buckles.

These high, barren hills showed little game, and that adept at getting out of range of rifle shot. Water too was scarce. On the fourth day they found a stream and followed it to its source—a spring trickling from a crevice in the rocks. They filled their empty canteens and went on, but there was the beginning of fright in them, for thirst is a thing that man is not made to laugh at, and there was a malevolence in these high, arid rocks which promised thirst a-plenty.

The tenth day saw the end of their water, and very nearly the end of their food. They were weary and footsore. The unrelenting mountain rock had cut their boots, ripped through to the flesh underneath, so that their progress was marked by red splotches.

They sat about a meager fire of dried brush, quick-burning and hard to replenish, smiling with a certain tightness at one another and playing variations on jokes that had begun to wear thin. Their own mental activity had begun to run shallow, burdened by the grueling necessities of climbing over rocks endlessly, of sliding down hill and pulling themselves laboriously up slopes, sweating one moment and chilled the next. Their mouths were always dry, and always there was that hollow tug of hunger in their bellies.

It is possible that on that night there might have been the beginning of acrimony in the feeble jokes they tossed at one another, if El Diablo had not made, then, his inevitable mistake. OUT OF the darkness above them, the sound of a displaced rock rattled through the night. They tensed, heads turning. A split second later a Winchester smacked its harsh, orange-spitting yell across the dark silence.

The bullet howled past Silver's face. Then, as the other rifles began to go, the camp was a blur of expert movement, as men rolled and whipped, gun-reaching, out of the circle of the firelight.

It was a mistake in more ways than one. The ambushers on the rocks above were no match for the men of the Hawk in this kind of fighting. They found themselves stalked by men who moved too silently to be heard, who shot with deadly accuracy just under unwary flashes, then rolled, snake-swift, away from their positions.

What had been intended to be an ambush fraught with terror and surprise, turned out to be a swift defeat. They fled wildly through the dark, leaving four of their men motionless on the rocks, and without inflicting any casualties at all among the group they had attacked.

But the thing was worth more than that. Nerves that had been drawing taut against one another relaxed abruptly in view of this common enemy. Men who had begun to doubt that there was any foe worth going after were convinced now that they had not suffered this grueling trip altogether in vain.

SILVER'S EYES held a grim glint of satisfaction the night after that unexpected attack. The way these Hawks of his worked together was apparent once more. It was not likely, he thought, that the rigors of these forbidding hills would threaten them with any kind of dissension again.

After that, they were slowed and harried by ambush after ambush. These guerrilla attacks were ineffective, for because of the lay of the land, they had to be conducted at long range, but they did more than slow Silver's party up. They starved it slowly and surely. What little hunting they had been able to do before was impossible now. Game has to be hunted only by one or two, not by a crowd. And to have sent hunters out under these circumstances would have been suicide for them.

The food they had taken with them had given out and now always the land led upward. The high, snow-covered peaks seemed almost to recede as they went on, rather than draw nearer. Always there was a new, barren valley to cross and another upslope to take.

The time came when the discovery of a chuckawalla, or even the small side-winding rattler of the hills was something to rejoice over, something to stay the savage hunger that ripped at their bellies. And always, ahead, was the lurking threat of death, silent, elusive, omnipresent.

Jim Clane, staring upward, red-eyed, to where in the far clear air a puff of white smoke lifted, cursed savagely. He did not even bother to take cover as the bullet screamed past overhead.

"Shoot, damn you!" he snarled at the invisible enemy. "You can't hit anythin'. But, by God, if I ever get you once over a pair of sights, you'll do the rest of your shootin' in hell!"

Magpie Myers smiled bleakly. "I'm afeered you'll wait a long time before you get a shot at one of them, Jim. Unless I'm guessin' plumb wrong, them are Yaqui Indians—an' a mountain tribe of 'em, at that. They don't aim to tangle with us, but just to wear us down. An' they can come purty nigh to doin' it. Them jaspers can live on nothin', go places a mountain goat would be skeered to put hoof on, an' hide theirself in country where a good-sized jackrabbit couldn't find cover."

Jim Clane's eyes looked momentarily maddened. "Hell an' hoppergrasses!" he burst out. "You don't have to tell me that. Ain't a jackrabbit ever born that'd try to hide in a bare hell like this, nor a goat neither. As to goats, we'd need to be goats with wings to git through them peaks ahead of us. By God—"

He broke off suddenly, looking startled and ashamed as he suddenly realized he was talking defeat.

Silver, listening, smiled. "Get it off your chest, Jim. You're no quitter, so you can afford to talk. And you're not saying anything more than the rest of us are thinking. Better have it out in the air than poisoning us inside."

Jim Clane opened his mouth, then closed it, abashed. Silver looked at the gaunt, ragged, starved crew around him. Then he said soberly: "All right, then I'll say it for you. We all know something about mountains, and this is about the worst mountain country any of us have ever seen. We're hungry, and there's no food anywhere. We're damn tired and cold, and there's no rest or warmth. We've pulled up our belts to the last notch, and that don't help even a little bit with the hell of hunger that gnaws under there, and don't quit.

"It'd be bad enough with just that. But the mountains ahead look worse than the ones behind. It's a hell of a question whether we can find a way to cross 'em, or whether we can last the crossin' out, even if we find a way. And with these Indians hanging on to us, it looks like we haven't got any chance at all. We can't hunt because of them, an' we can hardly sleep. Everything we do is slowed up. So that it looks like the half a chance we might have of lasting things out is cut into a tenth because of them."

SILVER STOPPED and looked behind him, and then ahead, his face a quiet, unrevealing mask.

"We've got a choice to make," he went on after a moment, "and now's the time it's got to be faced. If we turn now, we can maybe make it back. In fact, I think we *can* make it back, even if the Yaquis hang on our heels every minute of the way. But this is the far edge. If we don't turn back now, then there won't be any sense in turning back at all—because another day forward would add two days to goin' back, an' there's more than a few of us that wouldn't make it."

His glance swept them briefly, then he looked down at the lean backs of his hands, carefully avoiding their eyes. "God only knows what's ahead. Maybe it's starvation. Maybe it's freezing to death in some fast blizzard on the high peaks. Maybe it's a trap of El Diablo's—because there isn't any doubt that he's behind these Yaquis. In any case, it's not a thing I can ask any man to go on with. You've followed me where the risk was plenty, and not counted the cost. But there never has been a time when I led you knowingly into a place I didn't think there was a good chance of getting you out of. You'll have to decide yourselves whether you want to go ahead now. Talk it over, and put it to a vote. Then let me know what you've decided."

His quiet, queerly vibrant voice died out on the evening air and left an utter silence behind. No man spoke. No one rushed in with hot, unthinking words of loyalty and bravado. These were seasoned men, and they knew Silver Trent. If he was willing to admit that there was good sense in turning back, then only a fool would want to rush brashly ahead.

The silence continued a long moment—a moment during which the evening chill took on something of the cold, forbidding threat of the shadows that flicked down from the frozen peaks. A quality of supernatural silence and menace seemed to hover in the looming stillness of the rocks about them.

They looked up at the barren and hostile heights, and at the sky, its bright indifferent blue dimmed to a mysterious steeliness now in this twilight air. They were silent, feeling suddenly small, and lonely in this vast, arid immensity.

Then, like an omen, like an impersonal and contemptuous warning, the evening wind came down the steep, gloomy slopes before—a soft, whispering wind, the chill of death within it.

Its passing brought a sigh from those grim and deep-lined lips. Pablo, leaner than ever, the upflaming lines of his face like a death's head thinly fleshed, crossed himself suddenly.

"Such a vote is not hard to take," he said softly. "Those who wish to go back, let them stay quietly in their places—"

A pale, red-orange streak of fire flared against the far gloom, and cut him off. Something hit the dark rocks ahead of them with a squealing zip, then shrieked slantways to smack against the flat surface of a nearer rock. The wicked, keening report of a rifle sounded in their ears.

"And," Pablo went on uninterruptedly, "those who want to go on can come up and stand by me."

Jim Clane was nearest him, and stepped forward swiftly. In the group there was the beginning of a general stir. It was cut suddenly short by a jeering chuckle.

Pablo whirled on the sound, his eyes narrowed, his hand on the hilt of his belt-knife. When he found himself looking at Lars Johannsen, there was swift shock for one instant on his face, then the quiet, deadly threat was back again.

"You laugh, my friend?" he purred.

"Yah," Lars drawled. "I laugh at dat Jim. First thing I know, he'll tire himself out an' I haf to carry him."

Jim Clane shot him a furious glance, then grinned reluctantly. "Hell's back log'll be cold before you have to carry me, you durn Scandihoovian elephant. What's the matter, you string-halted yourself? Git up an' jine the party, a-fore I'm plumb ashamed of you."

"Like hell I vill get up," Lars returned placidly. "I am to move myself for dis Mexican ghost-hopper!" He leered insultingly at Pablo. "Dis is de trobble vit dis country—evert'ing is backwards. Dose who vant to go back, let dem get up an' go backwards. And all who vant to go forward let dem stay vhere dey are. Vy should ve all move for not'ing?"

EVEN PABLO grinned at Lars. Then he picked up a rock which was two feet in diameter and must have weighed fifty pounds. He heaved it, with a strength to which his thin body had no right. It would have hit Lars' stomach had not his big hands caught it as though it were a puff ball and tossed it aside.

"Get up, you great hunk of gringo lard," Pablo said, "or I will roll something down on you that you won't like."

Laughter ran through the group. Then Ricardo said, "Let him alone, Pablo. You know he is right. Let those who want to go back, move back. Why bother the rest of us?"

"Have it your way then," Pablo said, sobering. "But this is no joke. And neither Silver nor I will think the worse of any man who wants to go back."

He waited, but nobody moved. Then he shook himself impatiently. "Are you fools? Speak up. Do you want to die in these accursed mountains?"

"Nom de chien!" a voice exploded, "W'at is zis? Nobody is goin' to ron from zis Diablo. W'at is zis bad joke you make? Who can forget Mamzell Gracia, eh?"

It was Big Nose Beaujolais who spoke—a Big Nose Beaujolais scarcely recognizable even to his friends. Big Nose was accustomed to eat and drink not merely largely but enormously, so that his quick, steel-hard muscles were deceptively larded over. The layer of cushioning had grown even thicker since the loss of his leg. But not now.

A march that had worn two-legged men down wire-fine

had done more and worse to a maniac who tried to climb rocky mountains with a peg leg. Silver had tried to keep Big Nose from coming, but Silver might just as well have tried to whistle up the wind.

The fat was gone from Big Nose now. His skin hung in loose folds from his drawn face. His girth had shrunk so that he looked like a scarecrow in a fat man's baggy clothes. The rich wine color of his nose and cheeks had changed to a leaden gray, cross-hatched with fine black broken lines. And surreptitiously, whenever the crowd stopped for a rest he took off his wooden leg.

Everyone pretended not to notice that, respecting the secret he tried to keep. But scarcely anyone of them had failed to notice the stains on the padding which told that every step was rubbing his stump raw.

The crowd looked at him and grinned. Some laughed, but there was a certain shakiness in their laughter. The idea of the vote was suddenly, tacitly, abandoned, for the bad joke that Big Nose had said it was.

Silver turned away. He didn't have to look behind to see Big Nose was following. Nor any of the rest of them, either. But after a moment, he turned toward them again. When he spoke, his voice was gruff, to conceal the emotion in him.

"We'll turn back anyhow," he said brusquely.

They stared at him, unbelieving.

"Sometimes the easiest way to get forward is to go back-wards a little. I've got a notion that we might rid ourselves of our friends ahead."

The plan he had formed was risky enough, he knew. It would delay them, increase the marching they had to do, but it might work. If they could be free of worry, free to look for food, they'd have a better chance of getting through, even with the disadvantage of a couple of days' delay.

On the other hand, if the plan failed, they'd be no better off, and the loss of time would be serious. Silver knew that he would have to go on, in any case. Gracia was there, somewhere ahead, in Esteban Varro's power. But he knew, also, that if he went ahead, the others would come with them, say what he might.

Yet, if things were handled exactly right, he had a chance of success. The Yaquis, he knew, were near to savagery, and, like most savages, they could not endure success. If they saw that they had the white men on the run, they would lose their heads, press the pursuit too hard—and fall into a trap.

Silver picked out Magpie Myers, and, curiously, Beau Buchanan, as his first choice for the party that would trap the Yaquis.

MAGPIE WAS Apache-trained. Even as old as he was, he could move like a ghost, and there was a depth of fighting cunning in him which no one had ever fully plumbed. And Beau, his opposite, was almost as good. The immaculate and poker-faced gambler, who managed, even in this wilderness to look debonair and even dandified by comparison with his unkempt and disheveled companions, had an astonishing knowledge of plainscraft. He could read sign like an old scout, and take cover where there was no cover, like a plains Indian.

For a moment, Silver wondered if the three of them, himself

and Magpie and Beau would not be enough. He hesitated. Then Miguel said softly, "I was raised among the Yaquis, Silver."

Silver's eyes lighted. Miguel was new, but he had proven himself one of the best men in the crowd. He had a wife and child, who were even now at the Hawk's hideout, and he had risked them to give his services to Silver on that desperate night when the Hawk had gone to rescue Gracia, Padre Pete, Lars and Jim from El Diablo's ranch stronghold. If Miguel said this much, then he meant more. Silver nodded. "You also, Miguel."

Jim Clane looked pleadingly at Silver. "Listen, I'm a cowboy, but when I was a button, there was an Indian fighter that took me in hand, Yellow-finger Harvey. He—"

"The hell you say!" Magpie remarked. "Shucks, I knowed Yeller Finger. Warn't a better man in the mountains. Why, boy—"

Jim's eyes glowed. "You see, Silver?" he said eagerly. "I—"

Silver cut him off. "All right, Jim." Then he turned to the rest of the crowd. "That's plenty. Five is all I figure we need. Come on now, we're retreatin', and don't try to be clumsy about it, else the Yaquis will smell something. Act exactly like you would if you had decided to sneak off. Don't worry. They'll find us, all right."

That night, the Hawks silently slipped away—all of them but five.

Desperate with fatigue, their tired and starved bodies crying out for sleep, they stole through the night along the back-trail.

Slowly, under the glittering canopy of the night sky, they trudged on. Meanwhile, behind them, grinning and triumphant, the Yaqui shadows held to their heels. They did not attack, for to attack at night would be to expose themselves to close-range fighting with these mad gringos. They waited jubilantly until dawn. Then they meant to hurry even more closely, for now they had an advantage which they had not had before. Perhaps they could kill many of these men now. And, as the rest grew weak from starvation and exhaustion, they might kill all of them. What a tale then they could take back to the tyrant who owned the mines! And what a reward would be theirs!

But there were five of the gringos who were not with that wearily trudging crowd. Shadows that were one with the rocks, they watched the Yaquis steal by them.

Carefully, they held to cover.

When dawn came, the starved, worn, ragged crew of the Hawk, was deep in a high-walled canyon. Silver had planned that well. His photographic mind for the details of the country they passed through, had again coordinated with his perfect sense of timing.

Now, with the gray dawn light filling the canyon depths, the Hawks turned at bay.

CHAPTER 7
THE DERELICT LEGION

THE HAWKS did more than turn at bay—they advanced savagely to the attack.

But the Yaquis did not stand or fight. That was not their plan. They faded back into the sere landscape. Only one had the ill luck to expose himself, and he only to Doc Brimstone's rifle.

Three days before, he would have been safe enough, for the doctor's liquor had given out early in this trek, and as the bitter, exhausting days without a drink passed, Doc Brimstone had not only become a sagging-skinned, flesh-melted hulk like Big Nose, he had the shakes as well. Three days before, his rifle, in his jerking hands, would have been even more dangerous to his own men than to the Yaquis.

But during those three days, a change had taken place in Doc Brimstone. He had been silent before—with a dignity, and a severe reserve which forbade all comment on his condition. Then, the shaking had gradually gone away. The eyes that looked out of Brimstone's face now were clear. The night-twitching and the sharp cries which had disturbed the exhausted sleep of the others were gone.

Doc Brimstone, who, even drunk, was far from a bad shot, snapped his rifle to a steady shoulder and threw lead exactly through the middle of that one incautious Yaqui.

That was only the beginning. The Yaquis, over-confident as Silver believed that they would be, had all come into the canyon, except for four scouts whom they had sent, two on either side, to prowl the canyon heights.

But when they turned back, fleeing too fast for the comparatively clumsy-footed Hawks to follow them, they ran into something wholly unexpected—rifle fire, so swift, so utterly deadly, as to make their skill at dodging from rock to rock wholly useless. For Silver Trent was there ahead of them, and Magpie, and Beau Buchanan, and there were not three such riflemen anywhere from Mexico City to the country north of the Saskatchewan.

Beau Buchanan shot with the swift, incredible accuracy of a gambler dealing a cold deck. Magpie Myers, despite his age, could give you your choice of a rattler's eyes at a hundred yards and shoot out the one you picked. And Silver Trent was a better shot than either—which didn't seem possible, but had been proved.

So, in that chill mountain dawn, the Yaquis died. They would have surrendered, if that were their way of doing things. But as they would have given no quarter themselves, so it did not occur to them to think that surrender would do them any good. So they died, one by one, between the deadly trio in front of them, and the savage band that hurled themselves on their rear.

The four on the heights above, looking down, and ready to take flight, did some ruthless, inaccurate shooting at the small figures below them—the figures which pressed ruthlessly on the heels of their fleeing fellows.

On Miguel's side the two scouts were separated, and too much absorbed in the battle below them. One died silently with Miguel's knife in his ribs. The other was finished as he turned, with Miguel's thrown knife in his throat.

Miguel was to boast of that in his old age. It took great skill to creep up on two Yaquis like that.

Jim Clane was not so lucky. There were few better men than he in this shadowy warfare, but he did not think himself good enough to creep up on a Yaqui. Moreover, his two kept together. He took a chance and shot one dead with his rifle. At the crack of the shot, the other disappeared as though he had faded into thin air.

Jim's eyes widened and his mouth went taut. Now he had done it! If this man got past him he would take the word back— and new tormentors would be sent out to meet them. Silver had spoken of that, of the need of seeing that none got out alive.

Hastily he searched the terrain in front of him. He dared not attempt to remain hidden and wait. The Yaqui would be smart enough to circle wide. He'd lose him. The only recourse was to move forward swiftly, and at an angle, to cut the Indian off.

SWIFTLY, AS silently as a dawn shadow, Jim began to move. He knew that he was taking his life in his hands. Yet he hoped that the Indian would shoot at him. It would at least betray his position. Then, even though mortally hit, he might be able to get him.

He went forward fast, praying that his judgment of the terrain was good enough. In that tumbled landscape there was a chance that the Indian would take some other course, but Jim judged that he would go by a high, rock-shielded rampart, which ran diagonally away from the canyon toward the rear. He ran for it, angling to cut the Yaqui off.

The ridge of rock toward which he ran was about fifteen feet high and almost sheer. Jim reached it and flung himself up it, leaving his rifle below because he could not scale this natural wall with it.

He half expected to be killed as he swarmed up the wall, but emptiness greeted him at the top. He looked first to his left and his heart sank, for there was no sign of the Indian. Then, as he jerked to the right, a rifle cracked viciously and something slammed into his shoulder.

For an instant, the strength ran out of him, and he almost went down. Before his blurred gaze, he saw the Indian appear from behind a rock, and level his rifle to shoot again.

The range was close to a hundred yards—too far for a sixgun, and that was all that Jim had. His hand flashed to his bolstered Colt, thumbing its hammer back. The Yaqui shot again, and missed, but the bullet whined so close past Jim's head that it flicked skin from his earlobe.

The Yaqui levered his Winchester, not hurrying. Even at that distance, Jim could see the cold, savage grin on his face. The Yaqui knew that a short gun was useless at that range, and that his enemy was already wounded. It only remained to settle down and finish the thing off.

He knelt and aimed carefully.

But he was being a little overconfident. Jim Clane, to whom the knowledge of a sixgun was like a man's knowledge of the inner secrets of his own heart, was sighting fine along the sleek, blue-barreled Colt—not at the Yaqui, but just above the Yaqui's head. Then the gun kicked against his palm, and the heavy, smashing roar of it echoed, hammering back and forth between the rocks.

For an instant, the Yaqui stayed entirely motionless. Then his rifle barrel wobbled and dropped and his body followed it, toppling face forward. As he fell, Jim could see the black, gushing spot in the middle of his forehead.

Jim cursed. "Overjudged it," he muttered angrily. "A little more an' I'd shot over his head."

He had, as a matter of fact aimed above the Indian's head,

at an angle which he judged would make the bullet split his breastbone. Instead, he had hit more than a foot higher. It was an unforgivable error.

He walked up to the Yaqui and stood over him, his green eyes smouldering. He had to resist an impulse to kick the recumbent form. Jim Clane's self-esteem was hurt, and somebody was going to pay for it before he got through.

He searched the Indian and found a strip of dried meat—jerky. He snarled as his fingers clutched it. Wolf-eyed, almost slavering, he raised the meat to his mouth, then went still, remembering. For a moment he stood so, with his throat working, then he lowered the jerky and put it in his pocket. It would have to be saved to divide with the others, even if it had to be cut into such small pieces that it wouldn't do anybody any good.

He hoped that the others would find some meat of their own. That gave him an idea, and he went back to the other Yaqui he had killed. He found more jerky on that Indian and pocketed it. Then he turned, staggering a little, and went to find the rest of the gang. He felt stupidly weak, and supposed that it was because he had been shot. But the bone of his shoulder wasn't broken, so it couldn't be much of a wound. He guessed he must be getting soft. Otherwise, why would he have made that lousy shot?

HE CAME on a crowd jubilant with victory. They also had found dried meat, and not a Yaqui had escaped. Also, there had been almost no casualties. Enriquez had gotten a scratch along the ribs and Big Nose, bellowing curses, had broken the tip off his wooden leg, but that was all. Jim's wound was the most serious sustained by any of them.

Only Silver, perhaps, of all that ragged crew, was not rejoicing. His mind was already dealing with the future. It looked as though they had won a considerable victory, but there were still the mountains to be crossed and still the possibility that one or more of the Yaquis had been left behind and would carry the news to El Diablo.

The others, less reflective than Silver, were not quite so aware of the sinister cunning of the mind they had against them. An ordinary enemy would have sent his own followers to stop them and attempt to wipe them out. But not El Diablo. He had chosen for his purpose the one people who could live and move at ease in these mountains.

It happened that Silver had been able to outwit and destroy them, yet that did not end things as far as El Diablo was concerned. Silver knew that from now on they were not only at grips with the forces of nature, but with a mind so crooked and so subtle as to be almost unpredictable. Until they came to grips with the man himself, it would be like fighting a phantom, something evil and elusive and utterly deadly.

That was the main reason Silver's mouth was set a little grimly as they went forward again. There was another reason later. This march through the mountains proved to be worse than he had guessed.

Three days after the fight with the Yaquis, they were confronted by steep, granite heights that reared themselves

Had they any other leader but
Silver they would have broken
cover a hundred yards away.

almost a mile high. It seemed to them that not the Indians
themselves would have been able to scale them.

Silver looked at his men with anxious eyes. Enriquez and Jim
Clane were in the worst shape of all, even worse than Big Nose,

who had repaired his stump with a cutting from the last of the scrub oak they had found clinging forlornly to the rocks. But none of them looked as though he could stand this climb. Even with the opportunity of hunting, there had been little food, for game was almost nonexistent in this uptilted, barren land.

Silver went over to Jim Clane and looked down into the green indomitable eyes that glared out of a pinched and blue-lipped face.

"Can you do it, Jim?" he asked softly.

Jim glared at him. "Do it? What the hell are you askin' for?" he snarled. "What do you think you hired in me—a cripple?"

Silver's throat tightened, but he kept his face impassive. "Okay, son," he said lightly. "No offense. But stick close to me, will you?"

Jim looked at him, then grinned suddenly, with the swift charm which would come to leaven his pugnacity.

"Be yourself, will you?" he said. "Nobody's goin' to have to carry Jim Clane. If I can't make it, I'll stick around an' be good to the buzzards."

Off to one side, Big Nose Beaujolais had cocked a sharpened ear. Now he hooted. "By Gar! I am glad those damn buzzards don't eat watches. I will take dat leetle watch you carry, Jeem, when we leave you up dere."

Jim Clane snorted. "You'll be buzzard meat yourself, you bat-eared, one-legged Canuck, a long time before I give out."

Big Nose motioned toward the heights in front and then slapped his wooden leg. "Zis leetle peg will not be needed up

75

dere. Up dere you mus' climb wit' ze hank I pull myself up, but you have a bad shoulder. *Sapristi!* You are finish."

Jim grinned. "I'll bet you my watch against that wooden leg of your'n that I come out of it better than you do, Canuck."

"You have made a bet, *mon vieux!*" Big Nose grinned back at him.

SILVER TURNED on his heel suddenly and walked off. There never had been any fear to speak of in this big man, and he was ready enough to face death himself, yet he never could quite get used to the mettle of these men of his. When the pinch came and they showed their quality this way, it always caught at his throat.

Then the climb began—up battlemented rimrock, through short and narrow and glass-rocked passes that led only to more impossible climbing. They made a few miles a day, then dropped exhausted on bare harsh rock, too weary even to care that there was no more than fried lizard and sidewinder meat to make the evening meal.

Up, sick and weak and dizzy, they made their way, held together by the lasso ropes they had hoorawed Silver for bringing, asking if he aimed to dab his loop on a mountain goat. Now they scaled cliff faces where no mountain goat would have gone. Snows began and the cutting wind off the peaks ripped through their scant and torn clothing. They escaped freezing only by huddling together, and by getting up hour after hour and beating one another back to life. Then, in the bitter dawn, with the snow flurries in their faces and the hunger howling in their bellies, they moved on.

In front of the last snow-covered ridge Jim Clane gave out. He pitched forward on his pinched blue face onto the bare surface of a windswept rock.

At his side, a beak-nosed skeleton hobbling on a wooden leg pounced on him. "Ha! *Mon gars!* W'at I tell you, *hein!* You no good, *hein?*"

He began to heave, trying to get Jim on his back. Jim resisted, cursing feebly. But Big Nose set his jaw and managed to heave him onto his back. Then he fell down himself, his breath exploding outward as Jim's weight fell on him.

"Wat de hall is dis?" a patient voice demanded.

A huge pair of bony hands lifted Jim Clane and tossed him onto an enormous pair of emaciated shoulders, as lightly as though he had been a child.

"Come on, Frenchy," Lars Johanssen grinned. "W'at you try to do—play like you growed up?"

Big Nose scrambled up onto his peg leg. "Geev' me back my watch," he gasped, in feeble indignation.

Finally they made the top of the ridge, and Silver heaved a sudden great sigh of relief, for the slope down was not too steep. It was a possible descent.

A crystalline, driving snow was falling, and on the ridge the wind blew in his face hard enough to stop the breath in his nostrils. His gaze, seeking details of the downslope, checked suddenly. Through the fine snow, fifty yards away, a sudden, startled form faced him—a bighorn sheep!

Silver's Winchester whipped to his shoulder. The sheep swung, in a swift, effortless movement, hurtling to the cover of a nearby rock. But in that instant, Silver squeezed the trigger. It was as though the animal had been checked in mid-leap, then it plunged forward and lay motionless.

Silver's eyes blazed in sudden exultation. For this sheep was more than essential food—and now it was that—it was an omen, a piece of almost incredible luck. For the Bighorn is one of the wariest of all game animals, and to come on one that way was a piece of good fortune which made him feel that the endurance his men had shown had finally met with the approval of the gods of these bitter mountains....

They quartered the sheep and carried it down to the timber line so that they could cook it. It did not go very far with that famished crew, but at least it enabled them to go on. Even Jim Clane was able to walk by himself again after that.

They came finally down into the valley below, lean, grim, ragged, with the ferocity of hunger back of their eyes. And having accomplished the impossible, they would have small mercy for anyone who stood in their path now!

CHAPTER 8
ESCAPE FROM THE CORRAL

IT WAS queer to find the valley there. After the harsh and barren immensity they had crossed, the sight of green fertility seemed almost unbelievable. It was, in fact, a kind of freak of nature. For the valley was no more than ten miles long and five across, and it was enclosed on all sides by ramparts of arid rock—a gem-like oasis in a desert of granite.

78

Silver, his great frame gaunted down so that the cable-like muscles showed as separated ropes through the rents of his garments, led them on with the patient and wary caution of a scarred and starved old lobo. He had no way of knowing whether any word of their slaughter of the Yaquis had leaked out. He guessed that the Indians had been sent by El Diablo to delay them, prevent their getting food and cause them to perish among the high, barren peaks. Even hostile Yaquis would not have employed such tactics otherwise. And it was possible that one or more had escaped, unseen, to take the news below. In that case, they could expect trouble.

The snowstorm on the peaks, which had seemed another malignancy of nature at the time, now, showed itself as a blessing. Most certainly no one in the valley had been able to look up and see the scattered procession of black dots they made as they came down. And later the timber and brush had served to protect them. The thing to do now was to escape being seen until they knew something of the situation.

There was a town at the edge of the valley. They had glimpsed it as they came down. It might be a peaceable mountain village. On the other hand, it might....

It was, in reality, a Yaqui village, and one in what amounted to a queer sort of siege. It was occupied and under the rule of a rowdy and savage group of El Diablo's hirelings—insolent swaggerers, the kind of murderous scum that Esteban Varro needed for his service and who gravitated toward him as iron filings to a magnet.

El Diablo's men had been welcomed at first by these isolated and savage people, because they had brought a largesse of silver. The Indians had been impressed, and the men of fighting age had readily agreed to intercept the gringos who were said to be coming over the mountains and prevent them from ever reaching the valley.

El Diablo's men had seemed then to be a boon to the Indians, a source of riches—for a price was put on the head of each of Silver's men. The Yaquis had laughed in joy. They knew how helpless ordinary men were in their mountains. They would reap a rich reward, for they were certain that none of the coming strangers would reach the valley alive.

But, after the departure of the warriors, things had not gone so well. In possession, practically, of a village which now contained only old men, women and children, the visitors were neither amiable nor willing to pay for their keep. What had seemed like an influx of wealth, now became a burden, increasingly heavy.

In the first place, the amount of food these swaggerers required was appalling. The meager herds and gardens of the valley were hardly equal to the demand. The silver which they sometimes gave in return, and which the Indians had so greedily received in the beginning, now began to seem less valuable. The stuff could not, after all, be eaten. And the village was a long way from anywhere where it could be exchanged for the things they needed. It began to look as though their new riches would bring them famine.

Moreover, the visitors' initial friendliness began to wear thin very soon after the warriors had gone off into the mountains. They had the air of conquerors quartered on the peasantry of a defeated land. They commanded what they wanted, and when they were drunk enough to be generous, they paid. When they felt out of humor, they did not. Finally, by a kind of increase of habit or familiarity, they did not pay at all.

THE INDIANS grew sullen and frightened. But that was of little concern to their visitors. They had come on a mission which had promised to be difficult and dangerous, and now they found themselves in an extremely pleasant and comfortable position. The only thing the village of Tetuapetl lacked, from their point of view, was sufficient liquor, and this, after drinking up the native supply, they had remedied by sending a couple of couriers back to more favored lands for a donkey train of skins containing *tequila, aguardiente,* and *vino*. Meanwhile, they had nothing to do but wait until the Yaquis had finished their work for them. They had absorbed the Indian confidence in that regard, and looked on the matter as already accomplished.

The lean, long-headed, nervous Mexican who was their leader and who was called *El Lagarto,* the lizard, by reason of his physique and nature, was especially pleased with himself. Before long, he would have Silver Trent's head to carry in a sack back to Esteban Varro, and then he would have ten thousand dollars in gold for his own—a fortune which would make him a rich and powerful man. That was the reward El Diablo had offered to anyone who would kill Silver Trent.

It was also true of course, that he could get double that amount if he brought Silver in alive, to be tortured, but El Lagarto was a smart man and something of a philosopher. Capturing the Hawk was not a task that many men wished to attempt. No, he would be well enough content with the head—and ten thousand.

"Greed," he reflected, rubbing thin and nervous hands together, while his lipless mouth curved in a cruel and cunning smile, "greed is a siren who destroys the immoderate. Only a fool risks himself for a loaf, when half a loaf is sufficient."

It was perhaps on a similar principle that he attempted to take to himself the young wife of a warrior who was not there to protect her, passing by the attractive daughter of the village headman. While the headman was old, he still had a dangerous gleam in his eye.

It was unlucky that the woman's brother, a boy of fourteen, had the courage to attempt to protect her and was fast enough with his knife to wound El Lagarto before he was overpowered.

For this offense, of course, the boy had to be hanged. If an example was not made of him, the savages might get out of hand. In fact, maddened by the prospect of the boy's execution, one of the older men did make a frenzied and ineffectual attack. He also was hanged.

Nursing his cut arm, El Lagarto watched the executions with thin-lipped satisfaction. The spectacle of those two forms jerking at the end of their ropes—the firm-fleshed boy who had been so defiant-eyed and whose young face was so swollen and contorted now, and the old man whose thin legs kicked with such spasmodic feebleness—this spectacle was balm to his soul.

They made an amusing pair. "Hey! Dance in time, won't you?" El Lagarto yelled. "What's the matter, old man—can't your spindly shanks keep up with the young?"

This exquisite example of humor had a great success among El Diablo's followers. They roared with laughter, while the dance of the oldsters' shanks grew feebler and the villagers looked on with their eyes full of cowed hatred.

Afterward, when both forms were wholly still, El Lagarto was sufficiently exhilarated to command a feast of celebration. One of the few remaining valley beeves was killed and with it three young kids, to be barbecued.

Great fires burned down to coals in the pits and the spitted carcasses were hung and turned over them. When the meat was nearly done, skins of wine and liquor were brought out and the celebration began.

It showed signs of the being the least merry of those which the crew had so far held. Everybody was stimulated by this first open disciplining of the Yaquis, and also by a sense that they would not be here long after this.

"Drink your fill, *lobos mios,*" El Lagarto yelled, holding a skin of *tequila* aloft. "It is five weeks we are here. That means six weeks that these so-called Halcons have been trying to cross the mountains, for it took mounted couriers a week to bring us the news by the secret trail. By now they are starved, or dead at the hands of our Yaqui hirelings. Soon the Indians will be coming in with their heads, and then every man of you will be spending Don Esteban's good reward money. Drink to our friend, the Devil. We'll be leaving this god-forsaken valley before many days."

"*Por Dios!*" yelled one of his lieutenants, "it's a good thing, too. The fresh meat is giving out, and soon we'll be reduced to storage meat like that!" He pointed to the dangling figures of the old man and the boy.

A roar of drunken laughter greeted him, and the crowd of his followers yelled obscene and brutal jests as they moved toward the barbecued meat, which a voice now informed them was ready.

NO ONE of them had an eye for the gaunt forms that moved shadowy and panther-like down the brushy slope at the village edge. To these forms, the fragrant scent of roasted beef was a madness on the clear valley air. Likely enough, had they had any other leader but Silver, they would have burst cover a hundred yards away and taken their chances that these might be El Diablo's men. But Silver held them—held them creeping and silent until he himself was within twenty paces of the nearest celebrant.

Only a few rocks provided him with meager cover but even so he, with the others behind him, might have gotten into position so that the thing could have been carried off without bloodshed, had it not been for one of the Indian women. She caught a glimpse of those prowling forms and cried out, startled.

El Lagarto's head snapped toward the rocks, and he moved with the lightning, lizard-like speed which had helped to get him his name. He was on the other side of the cleared space where the barbecue was being held. His movements brought the carcass of the beef between him and the Hawk's guns. At the same time, he drew and fired.

It was the signal for an instant and murderous fight.

El Diablo's men, surprised and trapped, automatically went

to their guns. If they had realized whom they were fighting, or the disadvantage they were under, they might have surrendered at once. But there was no time to think. That first blast of gunfire set their gunhands in motion instinctively.

Instantly, the barbecue grounds were a seething hell of movement and sound. These men, whatever their other qualities, were trained fighters. They did not stand still to be shot at. They shot and moved, weaving, jumping for cover. And as they moved, they died—for hunger and exhaustion had not shaken the gunhand of the Hawks. Their minds and nerves were filled with a cold and savage clarity and their Colts were deadly.

One of El Lagarto's fighters screamed an agonized curse, and went down, clutching at a shattered hip. Another, racing for cover, stopped a slug that sent him face down into the coals of the barbecue pit. A third threw up his hands as though in surrender, with a gushing circle of red where the bridge of his nose had been.

Half a dozen more dropped before the idea of surrender really came. Then one man held up his hands, yelling, *"No mas! I give up!"*

Immediately, he was followed by another, and another. A second later, the firing had ceased and all those remaining had their hands in the air.

All but one! A commotion in the corral two hundred yards down the slope from the barbecue grounds caught Silver's attention. He cursed and began to run forward, but too late. The corral gate was open, and through the trees that half concealed it from view, Silver could see the horses racing out.

Behind them, the figure of a man appeared, lying along the neck of an unsaddled mount and yelling at the animals in front of him. It was El Lagarto. He had slid back, unnoticed in the confusion of the fight, and now he was driving off the horses.

CHAPTER 9
RETURN OF THE WOLF PACK

SILVER SNAPPED an ineffective shot at him, groaned and jumped for a fallen Winchester. But by the time he had placed himself in position to fire, the cavvy and their yelling wrangler were more than three hundred yards away and moving like the wind.

Silver hardly needed to be told that every horse in the valley was in that corral. By sheer bad luck they had come in at a time when the animals were not loose to graze. Yet it was more than luck which had gotten them out of the corral; it was quick, ruthless thinking. And Silver knew that in the leader of these men he had an adversary worthy of respect.

Blaming himself bitterly for not having made certain of the horses before he attacked, he turned back to his men.

His mouth was set grimly and there was shame in his eyes, but that crowd did not share his disappointment. They were busy tying up their prisoners and cheerfully cursing every knot that did not go right and kept them from the feast set before them.

Silver let them go to it, while he, with Magpie, who could speak some Yaqui, questioned the Indians about their situation. The savages, ignorant of the fact that all their warriors had died at Silver's hands, were inclined to be friendly and to look on the newcomers as deliverers.

When he was satisfied that they were safe for the moment, Silver and Magpie went back to the feast.

It was an occasion that no man in that starved crew would ever quite forget. The good, cordial wine warmed their cold and empty bellies, put a glow along their veins and a hot happiness in their minds and hearts. But it was the food that counted— great cuts of crisp-roasted juicy beef; tender, brown-crusted kid; corn and greens and potatoes from the valley farms. They wolfed it all, grinning at one another as they packed themselves. They gorged themselves gargantuanly, as befitted men who had accomplished the impossible, and were ready and willing to accomplish it again.

It was a great wonder that, with their starved stomachs, they did not give themselves acute indigestion.

Doc Brimstone, with a huge beaker of *tequila* in one hand and a three pound cut of steak in the other, warned them against it, in fact.

"You should take a little broth," he told them, "and then give your stomachs a rest before attempting even a small chop." He continued, giving the medical reasons for his advice and warning against the certain consequences of over-indulgence. But, between the steak and the *tequila* he was not able to make himself heard very well.

Only Lars Johanssen, holding a T-bone cut which might have done service for a regiment, paid him any heed. He had discovered a pail of the beef's blood, ready as an ingredient for

Above the gun-thunder came the
terrifying battle-cry of the Hawks.

soup. He seized it in one hand while he grabbed an ancient Yaqui with the other.

"Doc says I got to haf broth," he boomed to the uncomprehending Indian, "an' what Doc says goes, by Tor an' Wotan!"

He filled the remainder of the pail with *aguardiente* and made the Yaqui heat it over the bed of coals. "I ban drank dot when I finish my meat," he explained solemnly. And he did, between the beef and a haunch of kid.

"Dis doc," he said solemnly to the bug-eyed Yaqui, "is good

medico. You always do what he say, you be big man like me." He pounded himself on the chest.

Silver, doing his share as a journeyman eater and drinker, looked them over afterward with an appreciative grin. Not a man of them was sick, from a meal that ought to have killed them, and very few of them were noticeably drunk. Doc Brinkstone was, of course, and so was Big Nose Beaujolais. But not the rest of them.

The doctor was roaring a dissertation on the evils of overeating parsley, and interspersing it with appropriate ribald songs. Big Nose, whose great laugh had rung out like incidental music to the feast, was discovered later weeping over the last of beef bones, to which still clung some meat.

"My stomack she is shrank," he mourned tearfully. "No longer can Beeg Nose eat lak a man. Damn dose *sacré* mountains, I cannot eat her, dis meat."

AFTERWARD, THEY slept, with only Silver and Magpie and Pablo on guard, one following the other. Silver took the last trick, after the others had slept. He wondered at them, as he had done so often before. He wondered at Magpie, who looked fifty and might have been eighty or ninety, who woke him, soft-voiced and grinning, with hot coffee to open his eyes. And he wondered at Pablo, that muscled skeleton, whose flaming eyes had grown greater during these acid-testing days, but whose endurance never seemed to falter—Pablo, who had taken the first watch and who slept now quietly, profoundly and, somehow, alertly, ready to be wakened by Silver when the time came.

The time came soon. If they had had luck here, Silver would

have rested for a day or more, but now he wakened them at one o'clock in the morning, just four hours after they had gone to sleep.

They cursed him for it sleepily, and got under way.

"*Sacré Dieu!*" Big Nose bellowed. "My people say *"qui dors dine"*—who sleeps, dines, but this *salaud* of a Silver thinks 'who dines, sleeps!' By Gar, must we be waked in the middle of the night, just because we have had a little food?"

"Keep quiet, Canuck," Jim Clane grumbled. "If you'd look at that watch you won from me, you'd know it was past the middle of the night. If you don't watch your step, you'll bust that peg, and then I'll have to carry you an' win a peace of oak I don't want."

"Ha! Than to be carry by you, I rather be left wit' dose *sacré* prisoner dere," Big Nose snorted. "W'at happen to dem anyway?"

Silver, leading the way into the darkness, wondered a little himself what would happen to the prisoners. Perforce, he had left them to the mercy of the Yaquis. Would they take revenge for those who had been hanged? Or would they fear to harm them, because of what retribution might fall on the village? Or would the lone leader who had escaped with the cavvy return to free his own men?

Silver was inclined to believe that it would be this last which would happen. It would be easy for El Lagarto to drive the horses off into some draw in the mountains and wait for Silver and his men to leave the village. Then he could go back, free his own men, and riding, overtake the Hawks before they had gone far. And men traveling on foot would be at a serious disadvantage against mounted men. Not so long as they, the dismounted, made a stand under cover, but so long as they tried to travel.

From the swiftness and ruthlessness with which El Lagarto had acted, Silver guessed that that would be his plan. He was all the more sure of it because he knew that El Lagarto would not want to go back to Esteban Varro with a tale of failure. That, as El Lagarto knew, would be suicide.

That was Silver's reason for getting his men up after only four hours' sleep. From the Yaquis he had learned of the pass through the mountains, and he meant to cross the valley unobserved and take to the hills, not by the pass but by a harder route paralleling it.

That would delay El Lagarto, who would not dare to try to go back to his men until he was sure that the Hawks had left.

From the Yaquis also, Silver had learned other things—things that sounded like legends, like the products of an inflamed and frightened savage imagination. Yet they were things that by the very vigor and terror of their telling seemed to have the ring of truth.

The tale concerned a man who was neither human nor divine, but spawn of the devil and gifted with his infernal powers. This man kept a whole countryside under a reign of terror, and ground out of them the last farthing of their labor and savings in tribute. This man was nowhere and everywhere, so that little children waked screaming in their sleep for terror of him, and grown men breathed an air which they dared not call their own, for fear this hellish overlord would appear out of nowhere to snatch the breath from their lungs.

There was more—a tale so fantastic that it could not be believed—a tale which even the bravest of the Yaquis breathed in whispers with the fear written plain in their eyes. It was the story of the Mines of Hell, where men worked night and day, without ever seeing the face of the sun. Half-starved, pallid, miserable wretches, they dug out gold to enrich the coffers and increase the power of their master, El Diablo.

HEARING THESE tales, translating them, Magpie Myers had grinned at Silver in frank unbelief. But Silver himself was not so sure that there was not a great measure of truth in these reports.

It began to come to him that he had been an overtrusting fool. He had taken it for granted that Esteban Varro's power had been founded solidly in his great ranch beyond the Sangre badlands. When that ranch had been looted and El Diablo driven from it, he had assumed that Varro's power was broken. He had even believed that the shipment of silver which El Diablo had captured, was important to El Diablo in enabling to pay for arms for his attempted revolution.

But Silver saw suddenly that that belief had been naive and childish, and he wondered at himself for not having seen that that shipment could only have been a drop in the bucket, as far as the cost of the revolution was concerned. He wondered doubly at himself for not having realized that even the great Varro ranch could hardly have supplied all the money for that venture, even if the last head of cattle on it had been sold—and none, so far as he knew, had been sold.

No! Varro's power and the extent of his interests and his

wealth had been far greater than anybody had guessed. He had not been fool enough to try to conquer merely the country around Sangre. That was not valuable enough for the cost. Rather, he had had larger plans, of which Sangre constituted only the first step—plans which perhaps included the over-lordship of all Mexico.

Once that idea came into Silver's head, he became convinced of it with a sudden, startling clarity. He knew then that he had vastly underrated this adversary of his. It had not been possible for his sane mind to comprehend the possible ambitions of a soul distorted by hatred and rendered fundamentally insane by an egotism beyond the belief or experience of ordinary men. Now, he had begun to guess at the full extent, not only of Esteban Varro's wealth and power, but of his madness.

And with the realization came wonder. For so far, he, Silver, had been able to pit his puny power against the forces of this monster. So far, he, Silver, had come out on top in every one of their encounters—even in the beginning, when his smashing, vengeful lead had driven Varro earthward on the long past day when the tyrant had murdered Gracia's father and mother. Yet common sense told him that his luck could not last forever. If El Diablo's power in this harsh mountainous land was as great as it was said to be, or even a tenth that great, then the Hawks were in the greatest danger of their lives. They had undertaken a task which no other men in their right senses would have undertaken.

But the responsibility for their lives and their welfare was Silver's, and Silver's alone.

Silver's face was set in grim, harsh lines as he led them out that morning in the darkness across the valley bed. If what he had heard was true, he was like a child striking with a popgun against a murderous band armed to the teeth. Yet he had to go on. Gracia was there, somewhere ahead, in El Diablo's power. And Esteban Varro himself, Silver guessed, was ahead too, smiling evilly to himself, knowing that Silver would come, and expecting confidently that he would perish in one of the traps set for him, but knowing surely that if he lucked through the hands of the underlings he would only the more surely perish in the final trap of Varro's own stronghold.

Silver walked with the beginning of fear in his heart. A hatred boiled so fiercely in his brain that there was danger that all his cunning clarity of thought would be overwhelmed in its venomous bubbling. But, for this little time anyway, he remained sane.

After the start, that march across the valley became again like the silent prowling of wolves. Silver's swift, savage rebuke for any noise held them so. Under the chill, high twinkle of the stars they were a shadow drifting across the deeper shadow of the valley floor and up again along the slope of the far hill. Finally, the darkness of them disappeared into an up-going arroyo like smoke drawn into a chimney's maw.

CHAPTER 10
DEATH'S VOLUNTEER

IT WAS the last the valley of Tetuapetl's saw of Silver's crew of Hawks. It was the end of any man's seeing them, until three days later in the Valley de Argento.

Now, in darkness, waiting for moonrise, El Lagarto lay high on a rock over the trail they should have taken. He had waited for a night and day and a night again, his sleepless nerves jumping with impatience and growing anxiety. It was not until the second day that he drove the horses out of the box canyon where he had held them and, cursing, took the back trail. Even then, he made slow progress, for he did not want to abandon the horses. He had to ride ahead of them, and it was hard driving broncos from ahead.

By that time, Silver and his men had hit the trail behind him and were going on. Silver was driving his Hawks mercilessly, for he knew now that this whole thing was a matter of timing. Varro had not expected them to get through the mountains—and surely not so fast. Nor had he expected them, decimated and exhausted, to escape his men at Tetuapetl.

In any case, Varro would expect that El Lagarto would get him word by courier on a racing horse of his failure, if there was a failure. So Silver's chance lay in speed, and still more speed, relentless and driving.

The Hawks pushed on, starved once more and unutterably weary. Their nerves were savagely raw as they plunged into the valley of Argento, where El Diablo's third trap was laid. They came on it barefooted but with their bare and bleeding feet silent nonetheless. They did not approach by the trail where the careless guards were posted, but by a way which men should not have been able to take. In the clear, slanting light of sunset they looked over the lay of land ahead and formed their plans.

A ranch was situated in the center of this valley—and there were corrals with horses. The sight of horses put a gleam into their eyes and a quick exultation in their hearts. Every muscle in their tired legs ached for the feel of a saddle.

They came unseen at midnight to the corral. Then, even Silver's discipline failed. He could no longer hold them. They raced, almost fought for the lasso ropes that hung from saddles on the corral fence. Almost at once the corral was a milling, snorting confusion of caught or escaping horses.

A door of the ranch house burst open and a voice yelled, "*Que pasa?*" A window slammed open and there was another yelled question. The man at the doorway started forward, then changed his mind, his sixgun blasting thunder in the night, stabbing orange flame toward the dim figures at the corral.

Silver's instant lead slammed him backward toward the doorway. The startled shout of the man in the window turned off into a frightened squawk as a bullet singed his earlobe.

Cursing voices burst out in the ranch house, and in the bunkhouse to the left other guns began to bang.

Magpie Myers raced for the harness shed nearby. He fumbled, and then a match flared. Cloth and straw soaked in harness oil burst into flame. Magpie flung it toward the house. It sailed toward a back corner and nestled, blazing against the wood.

One of Varro's men ran for it and died in his tracks. After that no one dared.

The fire spread to the wood, licked upward, casting a weird and flickering light whose glow showed men in the windows and doorway and at the far corner of the house, and men surging pell-mell out of the door of the bunkhouse, blazing guns in their hands.

It showed also gaunt and ragged figures flinging themselves with blood-curdling yells onto the backs of unsaddled horses. And it made a paler orange of the stabbing gunflame that ripped death into the befuddled and scared defenders of that ranch.

They were more befuddled and scared than ever when yelling hellions on their own mounts bore down upon them with murder blasting from their howling muzzles.

Then, above the gun thunder, high-pitched and spine-chilling it came—the terrifying battle-cry of the Hawks.

"*A nos otros, Los Halcones!* Hell's Hawks for Trent!"

Running, shooting, weaving men stopped dead in their tracks, frozen by a sudden, almost superstitious terror. For they knew then. They knew!

What man in all that land had not heard that call—to his sorrow or his joy? Who, if his own ears had not heard it, had failed to hear it repeated in the telling of some tale? The very urchins in the village streets sent its high-pitched savagery skyward in their warlike games.

"*A nos otros, Los Halcones!* Hell's Hawks for Trent!"

The mountains knew it and the prairies. The stars gave it back in thin approving echo. The ghosts of the evil-hearted, it was believed, shuddered even yet to it in the byways of hell. In a thousand humble *casas* its echoing vibrations thrilled along the sleeping breasts of men and women who had good reason to love and bless it note for note.

"Hell's Hawks for Trent!"

Little hell in those Hawks for the decent and the kind, but plenty for those who rode with hell in their hearts.

And so this scum of the devil in Argento valley heard it, some of them not for the first time, and broke and ran, fearing it worse than the lead that sang around their ears or thunked into the bodies of their comrades.

That was the end of the raid.

WHEN DAWN came, Silver made as sure as he could that there was not an uncaught horse in the valley. Then the Hawks rode on—rested now and fed—to follow the trail they had learned of from a dying and fear-stricken man—the trail to the Mines of Hell.

They rode fast and hard, feeling better because they were in the saddle again. Silver drove them mercilessly. He could not tell how soon one of the escaped defenders might find a horse and get to El Diablo. He did not know what system of smoke signals Varro might have arranged. The only certainty was that if anything was to be accomplished, it had to be fast—so fast that Varro would be taken unaware again.

They pushed along the trail all that day, at a killing pace, without seeing any living thing. Silver let them rest for an hour at sunset while they ate cold grub. Then he got them, cursing, into the saddle again.

They rode all that night. Once, they came on a sleeping village, but Silver saw it before they were discovered and skirted it carefully.

Dawn found them weary, with the horses in bad shape. Again there was an hour's rest, and again they were in the saddle. This day their progress was slower, not only because the mounts were about done in, but because Silver led them a tortuous way, attempting to keep them always under cover. If their dying informant had told the truth, they were getting close to their destination. With each mile their danger increased.

Silver believed that the man had told the truth, for so far the trail had corresponded exactly to his complete description. Listening, Silver's mind, with its usual accurate vividness, had visualized every detail, so that he had felt almost as though he were riding over familiar country. Now that same synthesizing, photographic quality of his intelligence was busy with the details of the country ahead.

According to his calculation, they had covered between a hundred and forty and a hundred and fifty miles during the thirty-six hours they had been on the road. They still had some twenty-five miles ahead of them. It would take them all that night to make the ride, if they were lucky enough to make it at all.

The horses were already staggering with weariness, and would have to be rested frequently at night. The men were not in much better shape. That starvation trip over the mountains had done nothing to give them vitality for the work they had done since. They had slept little, marched hard and fought twice. Their red-rimmed eyes were sunken in gaunt faces drawn with utter weariness. The older they were, the more these days had taken toll of them. Magpie Myers, in particular, looked like a death's head.

Taking stock of him covertly, Silver's lips tightened with anxiety. Would he lose this best-loved and oldest of his followers because of the cruel need to get forward? Magpie's spidery, bandy-legged frame had always seemed to be made of whang leather and iron. But his resiliency wasn't equal to the brief rests and irregular feeding they had had. He did not snap back from fatigue the way the young men did.

For a moment, Silver considered ordering a night's rest. He knew that it was dangerous, that to do so would be to risk the lives of all of them. But he distrusted his judgment a little, because the nearer they got to El Diablo and the possible rescue of Gracia, the more fiercely impatience burned in his veins.

Then he shook his head. Magpie would survive one more night. And every moment of delay was dangerous. Regretfully, he ordered them on.

They might have to walk again, as it was, before they got where they were going. He had rated the horses along as skillfully as only he could do, but he saw signs that some of them, at least, would give out before the night was done. Some of them did. Dawn, nonetheless, found the Hawks on the ridge of a hill pocket which overlooked El Diablo's valley of riches.

The valley itself was little more than a pocket. Of irregular form, created, really, out of the confluence of three wide ravines, it was not much more than two miles in length by one in width.

On the low gentle slope of a highland between two of the ravines sprawled a town, remarkable in its extent and population for this high, remote mountain region. Its main street and most of its houses were low in the valley. Isolated log and adobe structures spread up the hill and ended before a wide space. This space formed a kind of rude lawn for a building which reared itself, gray-stoned and incredible.

IT WAS such a house as might have been met with on an eminence in some city where wealth and display were common, and even there it would have stood out in its magnificence and its solidity. Solidity—that was its chief characteristic.

Once the eye had passed over its magnificence and obvious luxury, the fortresslike strength of it struck on the mind like a sudden blow. From then on, a feeling oppressed the onlooker that this was in fact a fortification, and one over which brooded a curiously ominous air, as though it were the habitation of a man who knew himself to be in constant danger, yet was himself more dangerous and sinister than anything about him.

El Diablo's stronghold!

Looking at it, Silver felt a chill descend on his heart and mind. It was very nearly impregnable. An army could hardly hope to capture it. Those granite bastions were pierced for rifle fire. All about the structure, a wide open space, devoid of cover, would show attackers in a cruel light. Even at night, Silver guessed, El Diablo, would have arranged an illumination which would make it suicidal to try to cross that space.

There was no possible entrance, once the doors were closed. The windows were barred by steel; the doors themselves were of

Silver stood over the prostrate figure.

oak which looked, through Silver's field glass, formidably heavy and studded with steel.

Silver could see the circle of guards about the place. There were some two score of them, and from an auxiliary building, itself like a fortress, there swarmed into the morning light some half a hundred others—armed, bearing the visible mark of hired fighting men.

In the town below, the streets soon began to swarm with activity. Men who were obviously guards of some kind formed in a body and marched off to the right. Then other men appeared, some of them apparently simple folk, others with the brand of the killer on them. Silver knew there must be some two hundred hired fighters against whom his score of exhausted Hawks would have to fling themselves if need came.

For a moment he shut his eyes in an agony of despair. The choice with which he was confronted was one which no man could solve easily. He had either to risk the sacrifice of all his men, or to give up Gracia to her fate—or rather, to attempt to rescue her by himself.

Silver turned toward his Hawks.

"We rest here," he said crisply. "This pocket below the ridge is likely safe enough. It's the farther point in the valley away from the town. You'll post guards, changing every two hours, and you'll sleep. If anybody sees you and gives the alarm, you're to take the back trail fast. Don't stop until you've reached our hideout. The man who told us this trail told us also the way to find the secret trail across the mountains. Magpie and Pablo were both listening. They'll lead you. Nobody is to wait for me. I've got a plan that will keep me safe. Do you understand? Under no circumstances are you to wait for me, once you are discovered."

They looked at him in silence, a queer expression that might have been stubbornness, on their faces, but a look so overpowered by fatigue and the need for sleep as to be almost unreadable.

Silver turned away. He had taken boots for himself out of the loot of their two fights, and he had a shirt and trousers which were not torn to shreds. He really only needed to take off his boots to look at a distance, like a Mexican of the peon class.

He found Magpie at his elbow—a Magpie who, because of the utter exhaustion that rode him, looked like death itself.

"What are you up to?" he demanded, "You don't think you can get by in daylight like this, do you?"

Silver nodded. "There's a peasant hut down below where I figure I can get what I want," he said. "Don't worry about me, I'm not goin' to take any chances."

Pablo, at Magpie's side said softly, "Your eyes are still gray, you know."

"What of it?" Silver demanded irritably. "They aren't the only pair of gray eyes in Mexico. I've seen Yaqui Indians with blue ones. Quit worryin'. I'll take care of myself."

Magpie and Pablo exchanged a look, then Pablo shrugged and turned away.

"Well, good luck," Magpie said awkwardly.

Their manner put something like anger into Silver, but he had little time to think of it. The thrust of impatience in his blood drove him like a steam-driven piston.

CHAPTER 11
CHAINS OF THE DAMNED

H E WENT up over the ridge and down the slope under cover until he reached the adobe hut. A few words and some silver coins sent the man eagerly but on his mission of herb hunting. Three hours later, with more riches in his hand than he had ever dreamed of, he was lying bound and gagged some distance from his hut, while a big, brown-skinned peasant with a marked limp and one twisted shoulder higher than the other, went down the path toward town.

Silver knew that any stranger in this mountain town would be immediately noticed, so he was prepared for the instant curiosity which followed his passage through the streets. Except for a lackadaisical greeting to the folk he passed along the way, he made no attempt to explain his presence, and his manner discouraged conversation. He knew that he would be interviewed soon enough, and by men who would have no friendliness to him. But for once he had full confidence in his disguise.

His high-cheekboned face was no more than a deep brown parchment skin over bones. He looked starved and ragged and dirty. It was unlikely that anyone would suspect him. Even people who knew him well, might pass this emaciated tramp without recognizing Silver Trent. He made his way directly and with confidence to the town's main cantina.

As he walked, he solved for the first time the mystery that had been absorbing him. A narrow gully ran off the main street of this straggling town, and as he passed its mouth he saw that it opened out into a kind of funnel. Beyond it, the iron mass of the hill sloped up in an expanse pitted with burrow-like entrances. The mines!

Silver could see guards up there, walking about the cleared spaces where the entrances showed—guards armed to the teeth, with rifles, crossed cartridge belts, pistols and knives.

It was nearly noon when he entered the cantina, and it had already begun to fill up with hard-looking *hombres* who had come in for a drink before the midday *comida*, which many of them were about to have in the cantina itself. They were giving orders now to the proprietor, a fat, greasy, energetic man, with one blind eye.

Seeing him, the shadow of a smile tugged at Silver's lips. His observation about blue-eyed Mexicans was already proven. This man's eyes were approximately the color of well-skimmed milk.

Silver took a seat in the corner, with his back to the wall, conscious of the hard, questioning glances which were turned on him from every quarter of the smoke-filled room. He guessed that his presence there was resented, for the patrons were booted and spurred, of the arrogant, gunman type who seemed to form the bulk of the visible population of this town. They were the aristocracy—El Diablo's gun-fighters and guards—and they were not accustomed to having a bare-footed peon intrude into their bar.

Silver bore their scrutiny with a deceptive humility. Shortly, a lean, heavy-set and bleak-eyed man, with a slit of a mouth, swaggered over to him.

"Who are you, *hombre*, and what do you do here?" he asked without preamble.

Silver shrugged. "I have heard that there is work here, *Señor*," he said in the slurred, colloquial tongue of the hillman. "I would like to be a guard of the mines, for men say it pays well."

There was nothing in him to arouse suspicion, and the accent in which he spoke was perfect, not to be doubted, yet his questioner looked at him with a kind of narrow-eyed and wondering suspicion.

"You've got brass," he remarked, sneering, "What makes you think you are man enough to guard the mines?"

"I have fired a gun, several times, *Señor*," Silver told him earnestly. "And I am very quick with a knife."

The gunman laughed without mirth, and turned to the room at large. "He has fired a gun several times," he mimicked, "and he is very quick with a knife. *Carrao!* What will we have here next?"

Silver was silent.

The slit-mouthed man reached out toward him suddenly and knocked his hat from his head. Then he lashed out with first one hand and then the other.

Silver's head snapped from side to side as the hard palms smacked on his cheeks. For an instant, despite himself, murder blazed in his eyes and rioted along his veins. He fought it down, forcing into his expression the humility he had adopted as his role. "*Señor!*" he said, in bewildered protest.

But it was too late. The bully before him had seen that first flare in his eyes, and all his savage arrogance had been aroused by it.

"Dog!" he snarled, and his left hand whipped out. He took Silver's forearm, and dragged him to his feet.

IT WAS a mistaken movement. Silver's right hand flashed over, pinning the grip to his arm. His left hand twisted under and over, coming down on his assailant's wrist.

The swaggerer loosed a sharp cry, went irresistibly to his knees, to avoid a broken arm.

A startled gasp swept the room, then a low, cruel run of laughter, as the thin-lipped man remained helpless and writhing on his knees. Suddenly, Silver released him. In a movement almost too fast to see, he whipped a knife from his belt. It was at the gunman's throat before he had a chance to move from his knees.

"You see, *Señor*," Silver said softly, "I am very fast with a knife. If you would be willing to give me a job…?"

A quick gust of laughter blew around the room, and there were the beginnings of jeers and jokes at the expense of the helpless gunman. A pound of hoofs sounded down the street, a sliding flurry in the dust outside, and abruptly a lean, excited man burst into the room.

"Adolfo!" he burst out. "Adolfo Estrada—where is…?"

He broke off, staring, at the man on his knees before Silver. "Adolfo…."

Silver suddenly slid his knife back into his belt. It was no use to him now. This was El Lagarto!

"Los Halcones," the newcomer burst out. "Have they…?

Then his eyes lifted to Silver and widened, an almost superstitious terror coming into them. "Why this man—this man is—"

His hand ripped to his holstered Colt.

Silver's brain raced. Here was disaster, complete and absolute. With a curious regret he knew that he must kill this man. His right hand flicked like a lizard's tongue licking a fly, and blasted flame and thunder.

El Lagarto cried out, clasping a hand to his smashed shoulder. It was his left shoulder that was smashed, and that was only because of a belated and perhaps mistaken mercy of Silver's. He had thought that even if he killed this man, what had already been said was enough to make his own life forfeit in this town. So, at the final, ultimate instant, he had shifted his arm from the heart to the shoulder.

Instantly, the room was a wild confusion of moving men. Everyone's first instinctive reaction was to get out of range of that sudden gunfire. And every man's second reaction was to unlimber his own weapon and go to shooting.

Silver did not wait. He knew the value of surprise and fast action—and that he had little chance in this room crowded with enemies. He leaped for the window at his right, smashed a chair through it, and dived through after the chair.

He landed in the street and swung right, in the direction from which he had originally come. As his great body hit the dirt, he flicked to his feet and began to run, his gaunt limbs eating space in flashing, incredibly swift strides.

Behind him, a gun banged and a bullet whined viciously past his ear. Then his head snapped up and his heart dropped. Ahead of him were a column of perhaps two dozen men, marching two by two. He realized suddenly that they were the noon change of guards for the mine.

110

"Get him! Stop him! Kill him! It's Silver Trent," voices cried behind him, while gunfire cracked.

The column in front halted, startled. Rifles snapped to shoulders.

At his side, Silver saw the gully which led to the mines. Without hesitation, he ducked into it, just as a hail of bullets swept down the street from either end. He heard a cry behind him which told that the Diablo bullets had hit one or more of their own men.

Ahead of Silver, a startled cry sounded. The guards, hearing the firing and seeing his fleeing figure, whipped up their weapons. For an instant, he thought of going back, or of trying to climb the gully walls. Both were impossible. So instead, he charged ahead, running like a wild deer on the prod, and shooting as he ran.

One of the guards ahead dropped, gut-shot. Another went down with a shattered thighbone. The others jumped for cover. **SILVER PASSED** most of them, while their backs were turned. Like a rat bit running for a burrow, he dived into the nearest mine shaft.

He knew, even before the narrow darkness enclosed him, that he had trapped himself. But there had been no other way out. Step by step he had been driven into this blind alley—into this narrow and shadowy trap of death.

He found himself in a shaft which went into the hillside on a fairly gentle downward slope. Ahead of him, things loomed dim and vague, even to his night-sensitive eyes. Behind him, an incautious figure silhouetted itself against the light.

Silver heard sounds and voices from the darkness below and knew that he was caught between two forces. He raised his gun to fire at the figure which plunged into the shaft toward him from the upper ground. Then he checked his trigger finger. He must avoid advising those below of the real situation....

He returned his gun to its holster. His hand flashed toward his knife, whipped it over his shoulder and threw.

He could himself hear the faint whicker of it through the dark air of the shaft. Then there was a gurgling grunt ahead and the heavy sound of his pursuer's body falling. Another guard who had started into the shaft after his companion let out a startled oath and dodged back out of sight.

A turn of the shaft brought a glimmer of light from around another bend. He eased up and could hear voices, discussing what to do. The guards, evidently, had heard some echoes of the gunfire and excitement above ground. One of them wanted to investigate, but the other feared to leave his post.

"Stay here then," the first voice said. "I'm going to go up and find out. Two of us don't have to stay here to guard this ancient wreck!"

Silver shrank back against the wall as footsteps came toward the turn. A figure came around quickly. The beginning of a hoarse cry burst from the guard's throat at the sight of the huge figure looming there in the darkness. The cry broke off as Silver's fist smashed home to his jaw.

Silver caught his fall, and eased the unconscious body to the floor. Then he flashed around the corner, gun in hand.

The other guard was staring in a startled manner, but his reactions were too slow for the pantherine speed of the big figure that hurtled on him. Silver's gun barrel smacked his skull, and he went down.

Then Silver turned, his eyes widening with horror at sight of what was supposed to be a man cowering there against the shaft wall in the dim light of an overhead lantern. He saw an emaciated, pallid figure with a bristly beard. His head was covered with straggling yellow-white hair, and his trembling hands were cuffed together by a heavy length of chain.

He stared at Silver speechlessly, his eyes terrified, yet with the beginning of some strange wild hope in them.

CHAPTER 12
THE MINES OF HELL

"HAVE NO fear, old one," Silver said swiftly. "I will not harm you." The ancient figure goggled at him, his throat working in an attempt at speech.

"Who—who are you?" he got out at last.

"I am called Silver Trent. I—"

A croaking cry burst from the oldster's lips. "Silver Trent?"

"Sh-h!" Silver cautioned him. "I—"

The tattered, emaciated figure turned with sudden energy to a rock protruding from the wall in front of him. He seized it with surprising strength and pulled it toward him.

The rock came away, disclosing an entrance the size of a man's body.

"Gracia!" the feeble voice croaked. "Silver...!"

Silver's breath caught in his throat, and his pulses began to pound madly. Was he insane, or dreaming? Could it be that…?

Then suddenly she was there, her soft glad cry ringing in his ears, her pale and hollow-cheeked face looking out at him from the shadow.

"Silver! Silver! Oh, I thought you'd never get here!"

"Gracia!" His voice was hoarse, unbelieving.

Swiftly, gently, he pulled her through the aperture into his arms, held her in a fierce, incredulous embrace. Yet already his heart was beginning to sing with hope. The fact that he was trapped here in the mine seemed to have less significance now. It had brought him this luck. It might bring him still other unbelievable good fortune.

"We've been here so long," Gracia's voice was whispering brokenly in his ears. "Padre Pete fixed it so we could escape from El Diablo, but the only place we could run to was here. Dad…."

"Dad?" Silver looked at her startled.

Gracia's voice broke. "He was here! He's not dead, as you believed. El Diablo took us into the mines to see him, to torture me with the sight of him chained and laboring in this awful slavery. When you left with me, that time ten years ago, Dad was not dead—just as Varro was not. And one of Varro's friends came, and took them both away. Everybody believed that Dad had been burned up in the house along with Mother. Varro let them believe it—so you would be accused of their murder. He kept Dad prisoner, kept him in one place or another until these mines came into his possession, then he put Dad to work here, kept him underground and never let him see the light of day.

It was the beginning of Varro's slave labor—the beginning of these mines being called the Mines of Hell. Everybody, Varro's enemies, or mere harmless Indians who have offended him, he puts here. But they know the mine, better than El Diablo. There are secret places. When Padre Pete got me free, we had nowhere to run but here. Dad hid us. They've tortured him, because they suspected we might have come to him. He—"

A sharp cry from the old man at their side brought Silver around, whirling, crouching. A savage-faced Mexican stood behind him with rifle upraised to brain him. Silver moved with the swiftness of a mountain cat. He ducked under the gun, catching a paralyzing blow on the shoulder but driving his other fist into the Mexican's belly.

Instantly, the same fist grabbed the gun from his paralyzed right hand and slammed it against the man's skull. Silver stood over the prostrate figure.

Behind him there was another cry, then the biting crunch of steel on bone. His swift turn showed him the old man's manacled wrists still driving against the brainpan of a guard who must have crept up on them from the rear, and whose fingers clutched a knife which was driving for Silver's back.

The knife-wielder went down, senseless, and then, for the first time, Silver really looked into the face of the man who had saved his life. At the sight, his face went bleak, and an anger such as he had rarely felt flamed along his veins. Gracia's father! This broken wreck! Was it possible that the white-haired emaciated form before him was Phil Cary? Why Phil Cary couldn't be more than forty years old. This man looked a feeble eighty.

But there was no time to think of that now. A shuffling step behind him brought him around again, his gun lifting. Another guard stood there, indecisive, his rifle leveled, his finger tightening on the trigger.

THE WRECK that was Phil Cary grabbed at Silver's gun-arm. "No!" he shrieked frenziedly. But the hammer was already falling.

The guard, bug-eyed with some terror which Silver did not understand, took the slug square in the heart. But as the concussion slammed back and forth along the shaft, a queer thing happened. The Colt's muzzle-blast lifted, whipped along the roof of the shaft in a sizzling sheet of flame, then died out.

"Gas!" Phil Cary croaked. "You mustn't shoot in here. That is why he was afraid to shoot. You're likely to get an explosion that will blow us all to hell."

Silver drew a sudden sharp breath. He knew how close to death his mistake had put them all.

Back along the shaft down which he had lately come, there was a babble of frightened voices. Feet that had trampled, came to a sudden halt. Silver could visualize that passageway as it was now crowded with El Diablo's scared and desperate men. Fighting hand to hand with them, he would not have a chance. There had to be some other way out.

Phil Cary plucked at his sleeve. "Along the shaft, there's a back way out. Only some way, we've got to get by the guard in the main workings. There are a dozen of them."

Silver groaned inwardly, but started back. Then he stopped. "Padre Pete?" he asked sharply.

"Here, my son," a tranquil voice answered, and the priest's wan, benevolent face looked at him out of the hidden passage from where Gracia had come.

A moment later, all four were racing along the passage toward the main workings.

A guard showed at a bend of the shaft and Silver smashed him down. Another jumped out of nowhere, and Padre Pete's famous and surprising left hook put him to sleep.

Then they were around the bend and in the presence of the most amazing and horrifying sight Silver had ever seen. The shaft widened into a great gallery. And here, in the pale glow of half a hundred safety lanterns, toiled a crew such as few men's eyes had ever looked upon. Emaciated, filthy, long hair falling about cowed and brutalized faces, they were dressed in the tattered remnants of clothing which no longer even made a pretense of covering their pallid nakedness. They wielded picks and shovels which it seemed their pipestem arms could not support. Yet they wielded them with a weary and dogged strength.

In the center of the gallery were still other men, bony fingers clawed about the handles of crude barrows, into which the ore was shoveled. From there it was apparently carted toward the upper ground, and some mysterious destiny which Silver had not yet fathomed.

Yet from this sight, he understood much. These were old mines. They had been worked since before Coronado's time. They had been thought to be worked out and, with paid labor, the ore would have been barely profitable. Yet, worked by these slaves, unpaid and fed on a meager diet of boiled beans, the mines could still show a handsome profit—and at the same time satisfy the infinite depths of El Diablo's cruelty and sadism.

Silver's mind recoiled in horror at the sight, but the racing practical part of his intelligence was concerned with the dozen or more guards, armed with cruel, thonged whips and great machetes, who were posted along the line of the manacled workers.

They were staring, startled now and savage, at the gallery entrance, where Silver and the others stood.

Silver knew he would have to move fast. He did not see how, no matter how great his speed and ferocity, he could get past a dozen men armed with those keen-honed and deadly machetes. Yet behind him, were others, in overwhelming number—the guard from the outside.

He wondered why they were not, even now, on his heels. Then, muffled sounding far-off, there broke on his ears, the racketing sound of gunfire. Somewhere, somebody was shooting—a whole host of men. What had happened?

Then, thin, faint, high-pitched above the gun-thudding, a cry drifted to his ears and his heart stopped.

"A nos otros, Los Halcones! Silver! Hell's Hawks for Trent!"

He stood a moment with his head lifting. His great chest expanded and his throat tightened. They had disobeyed him, his Hawks!

He might have known it. It was not the first time. The fools! The crazy fools! Didn't they know that they were outnumbered ten to one?

Silver looked down to find Gracia's glowing joyous eyes lifted to him.

"Yes," he said huskily. "Yes. Come on!"

He turned and raced back along the shaft.

As he ran, the gun-thunder grew perceptibly louder. Were they coming down into the shaft? Of course, they would!

He cried out uselessly, his hoarse voice echoing. He could hear raucous, scared yells and pounding feet in front of him. Then it happened.

A detonation like the end of the world shook the walls of the shaft. A blast of air stopped Silver in midnight and tossed him backward as though he had not weighed more than a feather. A howling sheet of flame raced along the shaft, whipping backward toward the gallery.

SILVER LAY for an instant, stunned, his ringing ears oppressed by a contradictory and unbelievable silence. Then he became aware that his clothes were smouldering. He snapped to his feet and turned to Gracia. Her clothes were also on fire. He beat out that beginning flame, turned his attention to the others and himself.

Up the shaft, toward the outer air, there was silence, but behind him in the gallery, a sudden hell was loose. He ran that way. The workings were a scene of unutterable confusion. He saw a slave swing a pick and drive it into a guard's skull—all the way down to the neck. Then full realization came on him. The slaves had attacked their masters!

Sheer panic had no doubt motivated them in part; and the

fact that the guards had been knocked from their feet by the blast. From then on, it had been quick murder.

Silver felt a little sickened at the sights he saw, but there was a sternness in him, too, that recognized this as just retribution.

His voice cut through the howling mêlée as the last guard went down.

"You are free if you will be! Follow me!"

Phil Cary's quavering passionate voice lifted behind him. "It's Silver Trent. His men are outside. Who'll strike a blow for freedom?"

A wild, almost demented, savage yell lifted in response. The men caught up their picks and the dead guard's machetes and hammered each other's bonds loose. Then the whole tattered, pallid, skeleton mob of them—nearly a hundred in all—swarmed, yelling, along the passageway at Silver's heels.

Luck, incredibly good luck, would have it, the gas blast had not shaken down the rock roofing of the shaft. It was clear. They stumbled over the dead bodies of El Diablo's crew who had followed Silver into the mine. Then they were surging out into the open.

Silver's men, appalled at the thought of what they might have done to their leader, were fighting with El Diablo's other forces, but a party was already coming down the shaft to find out what had happened to those below. That party was lead by a wisp of a spidery, leathery man, whose face looked like death except for the blazing blue of the eyes in it. He moved with a savage energy which would have done credit to a youth of sixteen.

"Magpie!" The cry in Silver's throat was thick, at once relieved and shaken.

"Boy! Boy!" Magpie's tones quavered. "I thought—I was a-skeered...."

"Never touched us," Silver told him blithely. "But if you hadn't come... Come on, let's go!"

Outside, the deadly-shooting crowd of Silver's fighting men raised a great shout at the sight of him. Then they were going forward.

They were outnumbered, outnumbered impossibly, but the sheer exultant ferocity of their attack drove their enemies back. For the men of El Diablo were no more than paid fighters—jackals whose greatest savagery showed in easy murder, not in resistance to blazing, driving death at the hands of men who feared neither God nor devil, yet who shot as though the hand of heaven or hell itself trained their blasting muzzles!

And beside the Hawks was a sight to terrify almost any man—a screaming, hating, vengeance-bent mob of tattered ghosts, with picks and great knives and captured guns and even rocks in their hands. Mad with the thought of freedom, they lunged forward, almost insane with the outrush of long-curbed fury.

The men of El Diablo gave back and back, with Varro himself behind them. His raging, squalling voice tried to make them stand, but they retreated through the funnel mouth and into the streets of the town. Mounted men and men a-foot, all alike were unable to withstand the hell's ferocity of that attack.

Silver saw then that his crowd had come in mounted, and had

ridden their horses to the mouth of the mine itself. His horse was with them.

He flung himself into the saddle and led the charge down the bottleneck and up into the street. His great voice lifted in the high-pitched, terrifying battle-cry of the Hawks.

He drove through scrambling, stumbling, shooting, cursing men on foot, blasting deadly lead into those who stood in his path. Then he stormed up the street on the heels of the retreating mounted men.

AHEAD OF Silver, an evil, hollow-cheeked, vulturine face showed under a black sombrero. A gun lifted, spitting death at him. The shot whined past Silver's ear as he spurred his horse forward. This was El Diablo himself—this hunched, misshapen, black-cloaked figure who looked like a being come fresh from the nether world. This was Esteban Varro, whom Silver hated as he hated Hell itself. He was here—in his hands at last!

Steel-roweled, his horse lunged forward. A Varro man barred his path, and Silver's sixgun sent him from life to death.

Varro was wheeling toward a side street. Silver snapped a shot at him and cursed, as his hammer fell on an empty casing.

Varro's eyes flared sudden, hating triumph. He wheeled the great black stallion he rode and raised his gun, leveling it at Silver's heart. Silver's great wrist flicked. His empty gun sailed toward Varro. Varro flinched, his shot stabbing between Silver's arm and chest.

Then they were together, with Silver's horse driving past. His great arm shot out, caught El Diablo by the throat, lifting him from the saddle, as the man arced up a knife. The knife skittered away.

Behind Silver, a lizard-like man whirled, and the sixgun in his hand bucked and bellowed. Flame and a gigantic roar ripped along Silver's brain. The grip of his hand relaxed. He swayed in the saddle.

El Diablo hit the dust of the street catlike. His hunched, vulturine black body whirled, plunged between two buildings. SILVER MARKED that through the red haze and the yelling, stabbing pain which filled his mind. Clumsily, he tried to turn his horse, to put the animal through that narrow space where Varro had disappeared. But it was not possible.

Behind him, El Lagarto, who had shot him, chopped down the muzzle of his Colt to finish the job. In that split instant, gunflame lanced the evening air from the muzzle of a Colt held in the hand of a red-haired, green-eyed man, and El Lagarto's breath went out of him in an agonized gasp. He swayed outward in the saddle, plunged into the dust below.

Silver turned. A black flood was trying to sweep through the red of his mind, but he would not let it. Vaguely, he realized that he had gotten a bullet crease along the scalp and that a fraction of an inch more might have meant his death. But there was no time to think of that now. There was fighting still to be done—and Esteban Varro still to be gotten.

But suddenly, the fighting was over. The hirelings of the devil had had enough. Those who were not dead or wounded were racing for whatever safety they could find. It was a panic-stricken rout, as they were ridden down and harried by the Hawks who swooped and struck, leaving death in their path.

Yet, in that yelling confusion, Silver saw one thing that put a blackness of defeat in his heart—a hunched, black-clad figure, at the head of some two score fleeing riders, was racing toward the sanctuary of the graystone fortress above. Varro had found a new mount and had escaped.

For one raging moment, Silver was close to calling his men together to chase and attack those fugitives, even at the cost of trying to take Varro's impregnable house. But he knew that it would be suicide, and the murder of his own men. Half a dozen defenders could hold that place against an army, and Varro would have food enough for any siege. Moreover, there could be no siege. Varro's other followers would recover from their panic shortly, and return to renew their fight.

Silver's jaw set, his eyes bleak and bitter as full understanding hammered through his head. They had won, but this was only a temporary victory—for they were in Varro's country, and, if they stayed, they would be at his mercy.

There was only one thing to do now—take the backtrail, fast, before retaliation could hit them.

It was a bitter pill to swallow, but his men were worth more than any further victory could mean.

Silver turned swiftly in his saddle and saw them there—his Hawks, with the careless laughter of triumph on their lips. Sharply, with pain and joy, his eye ran over them—with pain because two were missing, Manuelo and Arturo—and with

124

an almost unbelieving joy because, wounded or not, the others were there.

Then his swift gaze went to a wan-faced girl, who sat a horse by the side of a tatterdemalion, pallid old man, and a swift exultation flooded him.

El Diablo had escaped him once more, but he, Silver, had won everything that really mattered.

"Let's go home, *hijos mios*," he said softly. "There'll be better wine at the next wedding."

POPULAR HERO PULPS **AVAILABLE NOW:**

THE SECRET 6
- ❏ #1: The Red Shadow $13.95
- ❏ #2: House of Walking Corpses $13.95
- ❏ #3: The Monster Murders $13.95
- ❏ #4: The Golden Alligator $13.95

OPERATOR 5
- ❏ #1: The Masked Invasion $13.95
- ❏ #2: The Invisible Empire $13.95
- ❏ #3: The Yellow Scourge $13.95
- ❏ #4: The Melting Death $13.95
- ❏ #5: Cavern of the Damned $13.95
- ❏ #6: Master of Broken Men $13.95
- ❏ #7: Invasion of the Dark Legions $13.95
- ❏ #8: The Green Death Mists $13.95
- ❏ #9: Legions of Starvation $13.95
- ❏ #10: The Red Invader $13.95
- ❏ #11: The League of War-Monsters $13.95
- ❏ #12: The Army of the Dead $13.95
- ❏ #13: March of the Flame Marauders $13.95
- ❏ #14: Blood Reign of the Dictator $13.95
- ❏ #15: Invasion of the Yellow Warlords $13.95
- ❏ #16: Legions of the Death Master $13.95
- ❏ #17: Hosts of the Flaming Death $13.95
- ❏ #18: Invasion of the Crimson Death Cult $13.95
- ❏ #19: Attack of the Blizzard Men $13.95
- ❏ #20: Scourge of the Invisible Death $13.95
- ❏ #21: Raiders of the Red Death $13.95

DUSTY AYRES AND HIS BATTLE BIRDS
- ❏ #1: Black Lightning! $13.95
- ❏ #2: Crimson Doom $13.95
- ❏ #3: The Purple Tornado $13.95
- ❏ #4: The Screaming Eye $13.95
- ❏ #5: The Green Thunderbolt $13.95
- ❏ #6: The Red Destroyer $13.95
- ❏ #7: The White Death $13.95
- ❏ #8: The Black Avenger $13.95
- ❏ #9: The Silver Typhoon $13.95
- ❏ #10: The Troposphere F-S $13.95
- ❏ #11: The Blue Cyclone $13.95
- ❏ #12: The Tesla Raiders $13.95

MAVERICKS
- ❏ #1: Five Against the Law $12.95
- ❏ #2: Mesquite Manhunters $12.95
- ❏ #3: Bait for the Lobo Pack $12.95
- ❏ #4: Doc Grimson's Outlaw Posse $12.95
- ❏ #5: Charlie Parr's Gunsmoke Cure $12.95

THE MYSTERIOUS WU FANG
- ❏ #1: The Case of the Six Coffins $12.95
- ❏ #2: The Case of the Scarlet Feather $12.95
- ❏ #3: The Case of the Yellow Mask $12.95
- ❏ #4: The Case of the Suicide Tomb $12.95
- ❏ #5: The Case of the Green Death $12.95
- ❏ #6: The Case of the Black Lotus $12.95
- ❏ #7: The Case of the Hidden Scourge $12.95

www.ingramcontent.com/pod-product-compliance
Lightning Source LLC
Chambersburg PA
CBHW052148170626
46812CB00004B/1646